TRIQUARTERLY
NEW WRITERS

Edited by
Reginald Gibbons & Susan Hahn

TRIQUARTERLY
NEW WRITERS

TRIQUARTERLY BOOKS
NORTHWESTERN UNIVERSITY PRESS

Evanston, Illinois

TriQuarterly Books
Northwestern University Press
Evanston, Illinois 60208-4210

Printed in the United States of America

ISBN 0-8101-5057-3 (CLOTH)
ISBN 0-8101-5058-1 (PAPER)

Library of Congress Cataloging-in-Publication Data

TriQuarterly new writers / edited by Reginald Gibbons & Susan Hahn.
    p.   cm.
        ISBN 0-8101-5057-3 (cloth : alk. paper). — ISBN 0-8101-5058-1
(pbk. : alk. paper)
        1. American literature—20th century. I. Gibbons, Reginald.
II. Hahn, Susan. III. TriQuarterly.
PS536.2.T75 1996
810.8'0054—dc20   96-3465
                                                                  CIP

The paper used in this publication meets the minimum
requirements of the American National Standard for
Information Sciences—Permanence of Paper for Printed
Library Materials, ANSI Z39.48-1984.

Contents

Acknowledgments

The authors would like to thank the editors of the following publications in which some of their pieces first appeared.

YOLANDA BARNES "Red Lipstick," *TriQuarterly;* "Sometimes Pain Waits," *Ploughshares.*

TAMMIE BOB "The Match (Blessed Is the Match)," *TriQuarterly.*

TERRI BROWN-DAVIDSON "Block Bébé" and "Three Marys," *TriQuarterly;* "Puppets," *The Ledge Poetry and Fiction Magazine;* "The Meatpacker's Dream," *Seattle Review;* "The Sexual Jackson Pollock," *New York Quarterly.*

EILEEN CHERRY "The Winter Barrel," *West Side Stories;* "Her Crowning Glory," *TriQuarterly.*

LORETTA COLLINS "Fetish," *TriQuarterly;* "El Día de los Muertos," "Soup," "Photo, Fable, Field Trip," *Missouri Review;* "Justine Has a Few Words for the Marquis de Sade," *Black Warrior Review.*

PAGE DOUGHERTY DELANO "Reba Talks of the August Strike," *West Branch;* "Electricity," *Tar River Poetry;* "Naming the Body," *Gettysburg Review;* "We Are All Girls," *River Styx.*

STEVE FAY "The Milkweed Parables," *TriQuarterly;* "Intimacy Lessons," *Newsletter Inago.*

WILLIAM LOIZEAUX: "The Greenskeeper," *TriQuarterly;* "Beside the Passaic," *Massachusetts Review,* reprinted in *A Good Deal: Selected Stories from the Massachusetts Review,* ed. Mary Heath and Fred Miller Robinson (Amherst: University

of Massachusetts Press, 1988), copyright © 1988 by The
Massachusetts Review.

DEAN SHAVIT: "Dressing the Dead," *Poet Lore;* "A Marriage,"
"In Her Kitchen," "Bar Mitzvah at the Western Wall,"
TriQuarterly.

CASSANDRA SMITH: "The Clock," *TriQuarterly;* "Mothers:
Three Stories," *Crescent Review.*

Red Lipstick

Lettie's coming.

She's coming. On her way.

That was her calling on the telephone. Telling me she'll be here soon.

Lettie.

Jesus Lord. So much to do.

"Who is this?" I said. "Who?" My voice harsh, not like me at all. That ringing phone had pulled me from my bed, that's how early it was, and I'm up by seven every morning. It's been that way for years. "Who?"

"Albee?" she said. I didn't know her voice. Imagine that. She spoke again, this time adding a weight to her words, leveling her tone with authority, calm. "Albertine."

"Lettie."

Lettie Lettie Lettie. Her name rolls along in my mind like a prayer, a curse. Like the singsong of a children's nursery rhyme, a chant to jump rope by: Here comes Lettie. Here she comes. Lettie. Lettie. My best-best friend. Lettie. Lettie. The one I loved. *Oh, but that was a long time ago.*

On her way back to me at last. I stood in the hallway after we hung up, wearing just a nightgown, my feet bare against the hallway floor, bumps on my arms and the back of my neck, a chill I was feeling and at the same time not feeling. I was bound to get sick, I was thinking, in spite of the flu shots. Nothing would save me. Such strange thoughts. About my heart, leaping so against my chest. It would jump out, I was certain, and I crossed my arms, trying to hold it back. All these bits jumbled inside me. Until I couldn't think at all, like the times now I am driving and suddenly people honk their horns at me, an ugly, rude chorus, when I have no idea what wrong I have done, making me stop in my tracks, same as the little brown rabbit startled in the woods, black eyes bright and body stiff, stopped in the middle of the intersection, and so nobody can go until I'm able to breathe again.

I have to reach for breath after Lettie calls. The weight of my crossed arms squeezed against my breasts. What a sight I would make for the woman doctor who worries about my blood pressure. Until I begin to rub my arms, my cheeks, the still rabbit coming back to life. Lettie's on her way and I have to prepare.

First move I make is to pull on my old housedress with the green and brown and yellow checkered squares, torn and stitched with safety pins beneath the right arm. Tie a kerchief around my head on the way to the front yard, the first sight that will greet Lettie. I carry the broom for sweeping the curb where dirt and slips of paper and soda cans have collected. But first the lawn. Down on hands and knees, my eyes narrowed and searching the grass for weeds, I crawl about, snatching at dandelions and crabgrass until green streaks stain my palms. When the walk catches my sight. My new walk that Mr. James in the green house on the corner just finished building without taking a penny. Mr. James with his pretty wife who nudges him to help the old widow down the street. He laid the walk just the way I asked, with bricks of different colors— pink, of course, but also coral and burgundy, yellow and green and gray. Like a crazy quilt, that's what I told him. Like Joseph's coat.

I squeeze my eyes tight and see Lettie strolling along that new walk. The way she was years ago, wearing one of her dresses, bright colored and the skirt swinging, brushing the back of her knees. Her plump cheeks and skin the shade of black plums. Her hats—the straw one with the scarves tied around the brim, the tails drifting down her back, and that man's hat tilted on her head, shadowing one eye. I see her hair dyed yellow. (How my Harald talked her down for that! "A woman with skin that black," he said, like it was some crime. "She's got no *business*.") I see triple strands of fake pearls slapping against her breasts as she stepped, and her lips, slick and shiny red, open and stretched across laughing teeth.

"Miz Clark?" I hear, and open my eyes. Sonya from across the street stands on my lawn. "Miz Clark?" she says. They all call me that. "How you doing today, Miz Clark?" they say. "You getting along all right, Miz Clark?" No longer Albertine. Nobody remembers Albertine but me. "Miz Clark?" Sonya is saying. "You doing OK, Miz Clark?" Her little boy and girl dressed in blue uniforms, on their way to the Christian school. They hold Sonya's hands and stare at me with dark brown eyes, the girl's hair all in braids and fastened with blue-and-white barrettes.

"You've been working hard," Sonya says. "I saw you." Her voice is weak, surprising because Sonya's a big woman. A big yellow woman. The way she fusses at me is how I imagine a daughter would. I know I should be thankful for neighbors like her. "Maybe you should rest," she says, but I just grin and pat her fleshy arm. Tell her to stop worrying. That's all I say. She wouldn't understand the rest, that I haven't felt so good in a long, long time.

■ Lettie never said what she wanted when she called. But I know. The same as how I know almost everything about Lettie. More, probably, than in those days we talked all the time. I know about that new house of hers and how each of her daughters turned out, about each wedding, each birth of a grandchild, each baptism, communion, graduation. I know about her boy, her baby. How his motorbike skidded on an oil-slicked road. He was nearly killed, and I know that nearly killed her. There are people who tell me these things, Essie in particular, but sometimes I wonder if I need them. I feel I would know no matter what. I would just know.

"Can I come over today, Albee?" she said. "I've got something to ask you." What answer possible, except "Of course, Lettie." All this time her words swirling in my mind until, finally, while working in the yard, their meaning comes to me, makes me sit back on my heels, although this causes great pain in my legs. Already my palms sting, my back hurts from all the pulling and stooping, but I have taken certain pleasure in all these aches, accepted any sufferings stemming from Lettie's visit as natural and expected. Now, at this moment, I don't feel a thing. "So that's what she wants," I say, then snap my mouth shut, in case Sonya's back across the street, watching.

There's a sickness eating through Lettie, Essie told me. She says it can't be fought. "They put her in the hospital time after time," Essie said. "But she always comes out." I could picture Essie on the other end of the telephone, shaking her head, black curls trembling. But I know better. Lettie is a cat. What else Essie tells me, that Lettie's alone. "Alonso's left her," she lowered her voice when she told me this, and on my end of the phone I nodded my head. My whole body nodding, my shoulders rocking back and forth, my toes in it too, tapping the floor. Ah, Alonso. Couldn't take any more. Lettie's carryings-on and her lies. Her arrogance. See there. I'm not the only one. "And the children," Essie said. "All gone too." That boy turned out no better than her. Traipsing around the country. Living with one woman after another. The twins, Claire and Carla. "They won't have nothing to do with her." Essie's tone hushed. Gleeful. "Won't even let her in their homes."

"It's payment due," I said. "Fortune's wheel turning round. All Lettie's deeds coming back to her. All the evil, all the lies, all that boozing, all her selfishness. All the suffering she's caused." I had to catch myself, listen to Essie's silence. It made me press my lips tight. Nobody wants to hear me talk that way.

Alone. That's why Lettie's coming back. She needs my help.

■ She'll be here soon, and so I move inside to the living room. She'll only pass through here; Lettie and I were never living-room friends. Still, I take my old dust rags and wipe the Beethoven bust on the piano. I grip the bench and lower myself one knee at a time to clean the instrument's feet, pushing my fingernail through the cloth to get at the dust in the carved ridges. I pour lemon oil on the coffee table and knead it into the wood. The centerpiece is an arrangement of silk flowers. It would be nice to replace it with a token from Lettie, but there is nothing. A punch bowl that Harald dropped years ago. When we were children I'd give Lettie presents. Little bracelets with dangling charms and necklaces with mustard seeds captured in glass balls. I stole from my mother's jewelry box a pin shaped like a bird with rhinestones in its breast. Lettie and I believed they were diamonds. How Mama whipped me when she found out. I gave Lettie the toy circus animals my daddy bought me when I was sick with chicken pox. Tiny, tiny things. When I shut my eyes now I can see them still: a lion, a monkey, a capped bear holding a little red ball. Lettie won't remember.

In the kitchen I fill a bucket with ammonia and hot water, sink my bare hands in and swirl the rag about. My fingers look strange, puffy, bloated, plain except for the wedding band I still wear though Harald's been gone, what, almost ten years. In the moment it takes to squeeze the rag my hands have turned a raw red. I was the fair-skinned one with the pretty hair. Lettie standing in the schoolyard behind me, playing with my ponytail, saying, "This is good stuff." Combing it with her fingers, plaiting it, dressing it with ribbons. She chose me, I remind myself as I clean. "Me." Wiping down the windowsill above the sink where I keep my pot of violets, the ceramic swan with the white, curved neck, the goldfish bowl. Harald's glasses. The last pair he owned, cracked in the brown frame. Oh, Harald never liked Lettie. He saw before I did. The way his face turned mean at the sight of her children here. But I didn't mind taking care of them, I tried to tell him, since we couldn't have any of our own. "Fool," he said. He knew what Lettie was doing, how she got those fancy hats and bottles of perfume cluttering her glass-topped vanity. "Fool," he said, and I thought he meant Alonso.

I want Lettie to see those glasses. And the drawings held by magnets to the refrigerator. Sonya's children colored those and signed them with love and kisses. I want Lettie to take note of the cabinets beneath the sink; Mr. James built those, yes, the same one who did the walk. And the large bowl on the table, let her see that, too, filled with figs and oranges and lemons and tomatoes and yellow squash. My neighbors pick these from their trees and gardens and carry them over in grease-stained paper bags. All this will show Lettie. "See, I have friends. See what my friends do for me. Lettie? Do you hear? I have a good life. I keep busy. I substitute teach and lunch twice a month with Essie. I attend all the meetings of the neighborhood block club, elected secretary two years in a row."

I shake my head. Standing in the middle of my kitchen, hands on hips, the rag dripping ammonia-water on the floor. I have no time for this, there is much more to do. A new, fresh tablecloth and the good curtains, yellow ones that match my kitchen. I need to get them down from the hall cabinet. I will fix tuna sandwiches, cut in triangles and trimmed of crusts, just how she likes, and put the rest of the coconut cake on the party platter with the red and yellow tulips decorating the border. When Lettie comes I will put on a pot of coffee. We used to sit at this very table and drink cup after cup.

Lettie making me laugh. If I had more time I would get on hands and knees and scrub the floor. I would wipe down the cabinet doors, the woodwork, the walls, till they're free of fingerprints and grime and grease. Sort through the cupboards, throw out the clutter, the excesses, and reline the shelves with fresh, new paper. I would clean this house to its bones, its soul. I would cook Lettie her favorite meal, gumbo with sausage and crab and shrimp. All that and more if I had the time. But a million years would not be enough to prepare for Lettie.

■ It's remarkable to me that I didn't know her voice. Of course, it's been several years since we spoke on the telephone or anywhere else. But that doesn't mean I had stopped hearing Lettie. No. I've heard her voice often. Still it follows me around, sits on my shoulder and whispers in my ear, pops up at the strangest times. Once I was slicing eggplant, and something about it, its deep black purpleness, I think, like Lettie's color, made me think of her, and I swear I heard her laughing. Another time I was humming some nonsense tune I made up as I leaned over the back porch sink washing my clothes, and her voice rose up over mine, singing one of those common, nasty songs she used to know. I must hear her in my sleep, too, because sometimes I wake in the night answering her.

Something to ask me, that's what she said, and that is just like Lettie. Seems like she was always wanting something from me. Never the other way around. Didn't Harald say that? And Essie? Oh, I was a good friend to her, everybody knows that. But I've learned my lesson now. I'm stronger than before. "Where are my little toy animals now?" My voice bounces against the tile walls of the bathroom. I hear in it the frantic pain of the old crazy woman filthily dressed who stands at the bus stop and shouts all her business. With trembling fingers I unbutton my old plaid dress and soap a washcloth to rub against the back of my neck, my ears, beneath my arms. Fill the basin with water and bring my face down.

People wondered after I let Lettie go. Prying, nudging questions. Essie tried to find out, oh, how she tried. She was so certain it was some one, huge thing. She questioned me about Lettie and my Harald; she knew how Lettie was. But I never answered. Let

Essie think whatever she wants, tell her tales. But this is how Lettie and I came to end.

The Christmas party at Essie's house and me still in my widow's black although Harald had been gone more than two years. That's how deeply I felt. Lettie should have known that. At this party I was sitting on Essie's flowered couch, a paper plate on my lap, listening to Chloe. I was eating one of those big black olives, nodding my head to whatever talk she was talking, when I heard Lettie's voice coming from the kitchen (who did not hear?), saying, "No, I don't think it's time Albertine stopped wearing black. Black suits Albertine." And then she laughed. I heard her laugh.

I went home after that and took off that black dress. I sat on my bed dressed only in my slip, my arms folded against the chilled night air, and began to think about Lettie and me. I combed through our history together.

Pulling memories like loose threads. One for the time after my third miscarriage when Lettie said to me, "Obviously the Lord doesn't intend for you to have babies, Albertine. Not every woman is meant to be a mother." A thread for the time creditors were after me, when I could have lost this home Harald and I worked so hard for (and I'll let you all know I never asked for a dime), and Lettie's answer: "Every tub must stand on its own bottom." Another for those two days Harald stayed in the hospital, those terrible last days, and she never came. Every insult, every hurt, every slight since childhood. All thought forgotten or excused or forgiven. All that I had chosen not to see. I sat there in the dark with goosebumps on my bare arms, pulling them from a place deep within me, weaving these threads together. Lettie had never been my friend. She had never loved me as I loved her.

■ The face I wash is old and full, skin loose and drooping beneath the chin, at the neck. Never have I been one of those women to worry about vanity, and I do not try to hide my age now. I pat on a little bit of powder and line my mouth with lipstick, pale pink, not red like Lettie. Once, foolishly, I asked Essie, "Does she ever mention me?" Anything would have pleased me, even spiteful words. "Does she?" And Essie waited, I could hear her thoughts weighing whether to spare me, before answering what I knew to be true. "No," she said. "Not once." I hold my brush with tight, curled fingers. My knuckles hurt. Twist my hair and pin it in two tightly wound coils.

At the closet I fumble through my hanging dresses. Which one? The black dress with the white polka dots. No. Eh heh. Nothing black today. The green one? The striped one? None of them seems right. Lettie will show up here in something red, hem swinging, slapping. She'll wear a hat with a feather sprouting out, or the brim trimmed with fur. Strutting up my walk without shame.

I could say no. That would serve her right. Laugh at Lettie when she asks for my help. Like she would do me. Leave her deserted. Yes. Exactly what I should do.

Such un-Christian thoughts ruling my mind as I stand before the closet. Finally, I shake my head and get back to business. It's the striped dress I finally choose.

■ Getting to be time now. She'll be here. Here. I rush over to press my dress, scorching my arm below the wrist. A bad burn, but the hurt will come later. For now I am free. Standing next to the ironing board, it takes long minutes to button up that dress. Lettie.

■ Sometime past two o'clock I wrap the sandwiches in waxed paper and push the plate far back in the refrigerator. Cover the cake and set it back on the counter. She should have been here two hours ago. Just like Lettie. To keep me waiting. And then I realize, such a horrible thought it makes me sink into one of the kitchen chairs. I brace my elbows against the table. She's not coming.

Has nothing changed?

I hear her first. Jump up and run to the window with loud thudding steps that shake the floor, stand behind the sheer yellow curtains. Lettie's here. That's her car. The gold Cadillac. I remember how she fussed and nagged until Alonso bought it, though they barely had money enough for a house to live in. I step back from the window, clap my hands, lift my feet, and turn in a circle. I have to do something with all this feeling bouncing inside me. "Lettie," I sing.

Does she ever think of the time she took me to the beach? I watched through the window that day, too, when she drove up in the Cadillac, new and gleaming then. "Let's go somewhere," she said, and I tugged the kerchief from my head. We drove, little

Alonso not even born yet and the twins mere toddlers, fussing in the backseat, nearly two hours along the coast to a mission town. Lettie wearing her straw hat that time with a yellow scarf tied around the brim, the tail fluttering out the window. We came to a beach with the prettiest, clearest water I've ever seen, white pebbles that hurt my stockinged feet.

Lettie left us behind, her two babies and me, to climb the rocks. She found herself a place to settle, her straight black skirt pulled up, showing her thighs, and a bottle of orange pop in one hand. Her hair still colored yellow then. Harald was right: a common-looking false blond. I remember the babies crawling over my stomach, their reaching, slapping hands in my face struggling for attention, when all I wanted was to stare at Lettie sitting so bold on her rock. Not seeing us at all. And I was thinking, "We ought to take these babies. Harald and me. Away from her. Raise them right." Treacherous thoughts, not like me at all, and I tried to shrug them off, a burdensome cloak around my shoulders, heavy, anchoring me. "We could run into the ocean," I whispered to those babies, gathered in my arms. "Disappear. Drown. She'd never know." And though it was hard, I waited and waited until it seemed enough time had passed so I could stand and call to her, wave her back to us, shouting, "Lettie. Lettie. Let's go home."

All the times I have remembered that day and what warning I should have taken. But I've learned. I won't be a fool again.

I hurry back to the window. "It's her. Lettie." Starting up my new walk. "What will she say about that?" I whisper. "My walk of different colors? About my dress? What cruel things?"

And then I see her. I see Lettie.

She's got skinny. Too skinny. Oh, that's a bad skinny.

A step closer to the window, my face pressed into the curtains. Where is her hat? She wears a wig, a cheap one, too obvious; it is brown with strands thick and straight as a horse's mane. She wears a black dress.

Black!

Lettie is dying.

Essie was right, I can see that now. This sickness has defeated her and now me, too. Robbed me of my Lettie. Left me empty-handed. What business have I got against this woman here? I leave the window, don't want to see anymore. Betrayed again.

Racing all around my kitchen, the nervous little brown rabbit. All the things that should give me comfort. I reach up and take Harald's glasses from the windowsill, hold them to my lips. But from them I get nothing. No power. Compared to Lettie, they're worthless. Everything in my pretty yellow kitchen, worthless.

So I walk back to the window and push the curtains aside. A ghost stands on my front porch, and inside myself I feel something falling. Falling.

"Lettie." Her name leaves my mouth in a wail. It carries through the glass pane and causes her to look my way. Through the window our eyes meet. Startled eyes, wondering, watchful. And then I see what I have been searching for all along. Her red lips. Red. Red. Nothing but red. Oh, Lettie's always worn the brightest red lipstick, ever since she was a girl and her mother couldn't slap her into stopping. *See there.*

At once I am laughing. *Lettie's here. Still. She hasn't left me. Not yet. Why, I'd bet anything, beneath that wig, she still dyes her hair blond. Scarce, nappy, yellow hairs. I'd bet my life.*

She stares at me. And then, slowly, smiles.

I let go of the curtain, fall back and lean myself against the wall. Breathless.

She will ask me for this favor. I know it, and without hesitation I will answer. Yes. Always yes. Anything to keep Lettie near.

And I begin to imagine the caring of Lettie. Shopping in the market, picking out the finest okra, the best green beans. For her. Plaiting Lettie's hair, pinning it up at night so she can sleep in comfort. Peeling potatoes to simmer in a stew to feed her. Washing her soiled underclothes. Bathing her, soaping and scrubbing her pathetic, racked limbs. Sitting by her bedside, squeezing her hand when she cries out in pain.

All these visions bring me joy. My victory.

Now I stand in the middle of my kitchen, alone on the checkered tile floor, and listen to the doorbell ring. Twice more I hear it, dainty and distant, but still I have trouble moving. Finally, after what seems an instant, what feels like my lifetime, I take my first step. On my way toward greeting Lettie.

Sometimes Pain Waits

We could tell it was him by the knock on the door. He would pound it, shaking the whole thing, causing the dogs in the backyard to bark and snarl and leap against the picket fence—a muddy-colored gate, really. I stayed near the back of the kitchen, hands pressed on my knees, all ashy and tarred-looking, peeked under the curtains of the kitchen window. "Shit." And just because I saw Mama looking at me sideways through slit eyes I said it again. "Sheeit. It's him." Everybody still as startled animals. Mama had been washing clothes in the sink on the back porch and suds crackled on her forearms. My sister Sherrie leaning against the doorway. We waited, but the knocking and barking and jumping just wouldn't quit. And, after a while, Mama snatched a dishcloth from the rack above the sink, wiping her arms as she walked-ran to the door to let Uncle Buddytooth in.

From the kitchen I could hear the high-note girlish voice my mother uses for greeting company: Hi, Brothertwo, Happy Easter. He didn't say anything about the delay, but then he never did.

Sherrie and me rolling our eyes and scrunching our faces at each other. Her pulling her fingers through her hair, Halloween orange color from that Sunsomething mess she streaked through it, and dancing about eyebrows that had been nearly plucked gone. Sherrie's older than me by almost three years but has never seemed it. We stayed out of sight 'til we heard Mama calling: Girls, come in here and say hello to your uncle.

He was sitting alone on the couch, straight backed, striped shadows across him caused by the sunlight filtering through the blinds. Arm draped awkward and stiff on the curled sofa arm, nothing but slipping plastic cover and empty space stretched out beside him. Mama half-slumped in one of the green chairs, leaning her head against a blue sweater I had left hanging over the back. She had pulled the red kerchief from her head and tugged at the ends with red, raw fingers.

I went up first, kissed Uncle Buddytooth quick on his scratchy cheek. A chicken peck. He smelled different, sort of old, spoiling.

While Sherrie took her turn I backed away, rushed to the only other chair in the living room. Didn't bother Sherrie none. She just strutted, that's the only word for it, over to Mama's chair, swinging her big butt, flashing the tip of her pink tongue at me, and perched real delicatelike on the arm. Made me wonder seriously why yellow-skinned, pretty-eyed Tom around the corner was always trying to talk to her instead of me.

The smell of cooking ham and black-eyed peas had trailed us into the living room, and I knew Mama and Sherrie were thinking same as me, wishing we could pack up that smell, hide it 'til he was gone. I knew I didn't want my Easter dinner spoiled by the sight of no-mannered him snatching at his food like one of the dogs, or hearing him fuss at Sherrie and me, telling us didn't we know better, you're supposed to stack the bread on a plate so a man doesn't have to always be asking for another piece.

No telling how long he would stay this time. I stretched out my arm, clicked on the TV, some silly Sunday-morning stuff, Popeye cartoons or something. Mama cutting her eyes at me; I turned down the sound. Just a pinch.

"How you been, Brothertwo? Been a while since we've seen you. You lookin' good." Mama's fingers sliding down the clean slice that parted her hair, checking the bobby pins that locked her two braided knots in place. She had what the family called good hair; thick and straight, slightly flaring. But she always wore it up or covered.

I looked him over, decided that was a lie. He had got skinny, too skinny. His neck was sunken and the dark, frayed suit he always wore hung loose. Even so, Uncle Buddytooth was still a powerful-looking man, the only one of my dead father's brothers and sisters to come out with strong, distinct African features. He was a huge man, tall, with eye-drawing black skin deep and shiny as freshly polished patent-leather shoes. Even with losing all that weight I saw he kept a potbelly, but that seemed withered and drooping, just like the rest of him.

In his huge, bony hands he cradled his Bible, a small black one with Holy Bible etched in fancy gold letters. The book had become so raggedy, the binding half torn off and the pages soiled with fingerprints and dirt. That book was in constant use because Uncle Buddytooth was a street preacher; one of those drunk-looking men and women standing at busy intersections, in front of downtown stores; one of those people waving their arms and spitting words about sin and praising Jesus; one of those people others hurry past, hide their faces from. That is what my uncle did.

"I'm doing just fine, Claire. Praise God."

"Uh-huh. Althea said you've been doing better. Said she got you to go to the clinic an—"

"That a lie! She tell you that? What a lie! That heifer ain't done a thing to help me. I wouldn't listen to her nohow. Liar! She tried to poison me. I told you about that, didn't I? Yes she did too. My own sister. She didn't tell you about that, now did she? But I tripped her up. Yes I did. Wouldn't eat nothin'. Just leave it there. On the plate. Every bite. You shoulda seen the act she put on then, Claire. All that fussin' and wailin'. And the *cry-ing*. Lord. Then the woman starts in again. On how maybe I should commit myself? Fiend. She-devil. Liar. I know what she's up to. Her and the rest. Supposed to be my family. Hummmph."

Mama clamping her lips tight, rubbing her forehead and eyes with raw-edged fingertips, waiting for the thunderstorm to rage by. I could tell she was searching for something safe to say. "Well—"

"I wish BJ was still here." Uncle Buddytooth stopped his haranguing and switched to a mournful tune. "If BJ was still alive wouldn't none of this be happening." He rubbed his eyes, red-splashed eyes, and I wondered if maybe he'd started up drinking again. Mama and Aunt Althea mentioned how he used to drink a lot before taking up Jesus.

I had been sneaking glances at the TV, looking down at my thighs spread out against the chair, reminding me of raw hot dogs. Looked anywhere but at him. Finally, I raised my eyes. He was staring right at me.

"How y'all doing in school?" he asked.

"Fine," I answered him, but turned my eyes back to the TV, tugged my fingers at the hems of my pink shorts. Every couple of minutes I would have to tear my thighs from the plastic seat cover, making a sucking, crackling noise.

"Oh, Noemi's doing real good." Mama was resurrected. "That one gets nothing but A's." In my mind I'm rolling my eyes. I hated to be bragged on for my schoolwork. Next thing I knew

Mama had jumped up, and in three steps, all the while talking in her high company voice, was at the mantel over a fireplace we never used, her eyes reading over a jambalaya of family pictures, school awards, and knickknacks arranged around a large, ornately framed picture of my father. Two fingers pinched together located and lifted the latest arrival, a third-place yellow ribbon I won in a school science fair, and she hurried over to gush to Uncle Buddytooth. I made some low noise in my throat, crossed my arms tight over my chest. Sherrie there twirling the ends of her hair, looking at something out the window. Made me wonder if Tom was passing by.

"Uh-huh." Uncle Buddytooth was bobbing his head, grinning, leaning out of the striped shadows to look at the picture of Daddy. "Smart. Like her daddy. He was smart too, growing up. Only one of us to make it. That's right. Only one. Got to be a doctor. Just like he said. Yessir." The smile didn't change, and it did. I thought I knew why. Mama had told us. Him and Daddy never got along. Well, *he* never got along. She told us how Uncle Buddytooth would bust into Daddy's office or come here to the house, talking loud and ugly and threatening until Daddy gave him money or whatever else he wanted. She said how Daddy had to get him out of trouble all the time, out of jail or whatever. Everybody knew, Mama told us, things like that is what made Daddy sick so young. Now I don't remember any of these things, but Mama claimed them to be true.

He leaned back again into the zebra pattern. "I know you've had your troubles, Claire. BJ dying with the children so little and all. But the Lord must have had a reason. Yes sir. He must have had a plan."

Then it started. Lord this; Jesus that. The recitin' and chantin' and dronin' on about Repentance and Ignorant People and God's Fury. Lord have mercy. Lord have mercy. Lord have mercy on these ignorant, common people who don't wanna know nothin'. I could feel a squeeze in my belly just waiting for him to open that Bible and begin quoting Scripture. Mama was massaging her temples, nodding her head, mumbling every few moments, "We know it, Brothertwo" or "Uh-huh, Brothertwo." Sherrie shuffling her seat on the chair arm. Me—I could make his voice distant, look sideways at the TV, or pick at a circle of dried spaghetti sauce on my shorts. But before long I felt something pricking at me. His voice. Something was wrong with it. I remembered it as a church-choir baritone, smooth and rich as melted chocolate. It sounded different, like he had to scrape the words from the sides of his throat, making them come out guttural and dead-sounding.

I looked at him again, closer. His eyes, once so black and strong and scary, were weak, barely standing out against a back-drop of watery red. His sunken face was dragging; every move of his was heavy and slow, as if his body was underwater. But it was his voice that scared me most of all.

■ I saw him once.
    I come to tell ya.
Preaching. I saw him preach once.
    I just come to tell ya.
He didn't see me, I'm pretty sure.
    Listen. I'm just about finished now.
I was with Esther, waiting on the No. 5 Express going down-town. I heard his voice first, felt a chill set in my face. Finally turning, seeing that it was him standing a little ways down the block. He was standing there, high on his toes, on Martin Luther King Boulevard.

His voice was not tired then: *I tell ya one thinng-ga. I try to bring you good noos-sa. I'm not preaching about religion. Nooo. I'm preaching about SALVATION.*

Different than his living-room sermons. It was music: a sor-rowful alto rocking, holding. Words coming out. Stop and go. Words spit out, spilling out: kissed words; hushed words, swelling; shouted words screamed in a raspy voice. One hand gripping that familiar Bible. Arms waving, pointing, reaching. Body jerking, dancing. Legs skipping. All to the melody of his chants. What is he doing? Face earnest and strained and wet.

NO. Religion can't save ya. Looking back, worrying about it can't help ya. Ya got to look forward-da. I'm telling ya. Ya got to look up-pa. Not to man-made idols. NO! LooktaGodLookta God LooktaGod. LIVE. According to the Word. I'm telling ya.

Squeezing myself on the green wooden bench, peeking over a mean-looking lady sitting next to me to watch him, never looking too long, too scared that my staring would draw his eyes to mine.

Ducking behind the mean lady every time he turned my way. Did he see me?

Still, I could not keep myself from watching. People trotting past him, stepping out of their paths, away from him. They kept their heads down.

I tell ya thisss-sa. If you go to your Bible you will find-da SAL-VATION.

People trotting by.

I tell ya. I'm just telling ya.

Him stretching out that big hand, reaching out but holding back, too. After a while his face grew twisted, ugly. "Sinners," he spat. Then wailed. "Sinners. REPENT."

Something must have shown on my face. Esther was looking at me with a question on her face, one eyebrow arched high, just like she practiced. The face softening; Esther jerking her chin toward Uncle Buddytooth. "Just another crazy niggah, huh?" I got up, pressed my lips tight. The bus was coming. Esther seeing me look at him again. "You plannin' on gettin' religion or something?"

"You crazy?" My voice sounding to me like it was being squeezed through a strainer. I jumped through the unfolded accordion doors of the bus, found a seat next to a grinning Chicano with missing teeth, and made myself not look back.

■ Uncle Buddytooth stopped his sermon. His face and withered chicken neck were all wet, and he reached two fingers into his breast pocket, drawing out a cloth handkerchief, clean and white. Draping the cloth across his large palm he brought his wet black face down, buried it in the starched whiteness and rubbed.

"How y'all enjoying your Easter?" Crumpling the handkerchief now. Blowing his nose with rude, loud snorts.

We all got real quiet. I remember thinking: Jesus, please don't let him ask to stay for dinner. Please, God. And even though it was a silent prayer I made sure not to look at Uncle Buddytooth.

When he spoke his voice squeezed out low and small, and he bobbed his head softly. "Smells good." Mama nodding her head, too, at nothing really, and Sherrie tugging, tugging at her hair.

"I had wanted to take y'all out. But, well, my checks haven't come yet. Nice place too, Claire. Good cooking."

"Oh, that's all right, Brothertwo. You don't have to be spending your money on us anyhow. You have little enou—"

"I know I don't have to. I didn't say I had to." Something in his voice made us all silent.

He got quiet, too, just sat there, waiting, his thumb stroking the Bible. After a few moments, "Could . . . somebody . . . get . . . me . . . a . . . glass . . . of . . . water? PLEASE." Uncle Buddytooth asked in a way that made Sherrie and me stop sneaking silly looks and jerk our heads to face him with startled eyes. Sherrie was quicker than me that time, leaping up and leaving me there.

We could hear pot covers rattling and clanging; Sherrie taking her time, checking the dinner, probably lowering or cutting off the cooking fires. Mama talking to him in her high-pitched voice, but I'm not listening to the words. What is wrong with him, I was thinking, to make us so mean?

About this time Uncle Buddytooth erupted—a fit of quaking coughs that shook Mama and me, too, made us snap our eyes to him, scared. Mama called to Sherrie (and now her true voice came back, the one I knew) to Hurry Up With That Water Now, and she rushed to the kitchen with pounding steps. The moment Mama left he settled down again. Almost quiet now, just his chest heaving. And then I realized we were alone. I folded my arms and crossed my legs, tried to make myself small; turned my eyes away but saw him there just the same. When I looked at him, finally, he was watching me.

"Does it hurt?" I wanted to know, and his sickly eyes studied me.

"Sometimes," he answered. "Always when I least expect. Sometimes it waits. Pain. And comes later. Keeps me from getting a full night's sleep." A few more coughs came; ugly and scraping. When they were finished, he tried to smile. "You know what? You look just like your daddy. Ha. Just the picture. Guess you hear that enough, huh?"

He was leaning forward, watching me, lips holding on to the smile. But I'm not ready to give anything. Uncle Buddytooth fell back, his black bony fingers spread wide over his knees.

Mama and Sherrie back, standing there I don't know how long; Sherrie holding a long, pink glass of water. Uncle Buddytooth standing, taking the glass. Him stretching to his full, massive height, leaning back his head, tilting the glass, drinking the water in three noisy swallows. Three tight knots I could almost see traveling down his throat.

He hugged the Bible to his chest. "Y'all enjoy your Easter dinner now," he said. "I was just paying a visit." He waited at the door, briefly. And then he was gone. All of us—Mama, Sherrie, and me—standing there; must have been just a minute. We listened to him leave, the door slammed, and the dogs barking, snarling, and leaping again.

The Fate of Great Love

When she was eleven Ruthie discovered romantic love, not as a participant but as an inflamed, yearning spectator. The affair featured her cousin Elisabeth, home for Thanksgiving from her first year at Brandeis University. Thanksgiving was at the home of Elisabeth's parents, Uncle Sol and Aunt Leonora, because of all the family, only they already owned a house with enough room to seat everyone, all the aunts and near-aunts. In America doctors made money quickly, Mommy and Daddy remarked more than once, even not very good doctors like Uncle Sol, who was unsure from one moment to the next whether he was in Poland or Germany or Cleveland, whether he was hiding from Nazis or searching his closet for a tie.

As a result, he had to be a doctor in the Hough area, where the Negroes lived, which Ruthie thought was too bad for them. But what could you do, Daddy would shrug, shaking his head as if it were sad for him to once again have to explain to Ruthie an example of the world's harshness. Most doctors wouldn't practice in that neighborhood, and even a doctor like Sol was better for those people than no doctor at all.

And, Mommy would add, lowering her eyelashes to cast a tragic shadow over her cheekbones, another sad fact was that in America learning was not respected as it was in Europe. That was why it took a long time for a professor like Daddy to earn enough money for a house, especially since they'd started out with nothing, which was what everyone had brought from Europe, *nichts*, because Hitler had stolen everything except their lives, which, of course, were all that mattered, finally. (A sour note in Mommy's voice suggested that now, with life long out of jeopardy, she again longed for what was taken.) But when Daddy got tenure, soon,

Mommy said, their family would have a house, although probably not as big as Uncle Sol's and certainly not as grand as the ones lost in Europe.

Everybody was eager to see Elisabeth during her first visit home from Brandeis, such a first-class school, comparable to Heidelberg, the Sorbonne, Oxford, or Harvard here in America—but for Jews, named for a Jew, a Judge Brandeis. Their European accents pronounced it "Brendt-Ice," making Ruthie, who understood German, picture burning ice, a frozen pond aflame. (It was the pond in Boston Commons, portrayed in a postcard Elisabeth had sent her. The blaze consumed ice skaters and swan boats; it leaped snowdrifts to scorch and blacken ivied buildings, the Jewish Supreme Court judge, and, most horribly, Elisabeth, as if her attendance at this important college were connected to the family's suffering in Europe at the hands of the Nazis twenty years earlier.)

She was bringing a boy home with her, already . . . one aunt telephoned another, spreading the news. What could that mean, after such a short time? Ach, what happens when children leave home: shock and heartache! Why did Sol and Leonora allow her to study so far away, knowing their days would bloat, listless and flabby, with Elisabeth gone? Uncle Sol had announced that his daughter would study at the best place for her chosen field, psychology, just as he had gone from Poland to Germany as a young man to study medicine. He admitted, teeth glinting gold beneath his mustache, that he had made a little money in America, could afford to send his daughter to any college she wished . . . it was not the nineteenth century anymore, when girls had to stay home until they married.

Who would think Sol capable of such new ideas, the way he constantly reentered his terrible past, twisting every emblem into a swastika, ranting about the evil world that tolerated and even encouraged atrocities, invoking the words and deeds of his murdered parents, brothers, sisters, friends, as if he had seen them just yesterday or expected them to drop by tomorrow. Yet he did see that Elisabeth was not part of that world, even though she had been born in the refugee camp Bergen-Belsen, a tulip poking through foul refuse, a diamond swept from the poisonous cinders of the former death camp.

Of course boys adored Elisabeth, the family knew any boy

would want to pursue her . . . but to bring him here right away? Could it be serious already? Aunt Leonora didn't say, or didn't know; she had always refrained from interfering too much in Elisabeth's activities, raising her daughter "the way it's done in America," as if those words were an antidote against the poisons that had polluted her own life. In contrast, Mommy, who had determined to leave Europe's awfulness behind (perhaps because her wartime life of pretense and hiding had taught her to adapt), believed she should have a hand in every aspect of her children's lives. Why shouldn't they benefit from her great experience? For example, she often advised Ruthie that with careful grooming and a sweet smile she would not feel so inferior to her older cousin.

"You shouldn't be jealous of Elisabeth's blond hair, or all her prizes: debating, writing, cheerleading. You're as smart as she is—what you should watch is how she combines her brains with sweetness, with humor to convince people that she's the most beautiful, the most talented. Femininity can be learned. Do what she does. Then when you're older you'll have many boyfriends, too."

Ruthie knew this was untrue; she could no more become like Elisabeth by observing her than she could acquire the delicacy of a hummingbird by observing it. (She was proud of this particularly elegant metaphor, but wasn't ready to say it aloud yet . . . it was possible that Mommy would laugh.) Anyhow, she wasn't jealous of her cousin, any more than she was jealous of a Mozart symphony—for envy there had to be some basis of comparison, and between herself and Elisabeth she could find none. Like the rest of the world, she idolized and treasured her cousin. Still, she could see how Mommy, so lovely and clever, would expect to have a daughter like Elisabeth instead of pudgy, stringy-haired Ruthie, whose dour face, whose aura of gravity, could easily be imagined belonging to a daughter of Aunt Leonora.

Ruthie thought that if she were Elisabeth, she, too, would want to go to college as far away as possible to escape her gloomy parents, although her cousin had never expressed or implied such a wish, even during the intimate times when she'd invited Ruthie into her room, allowing her younger cousin to examine her fascinating possessions: teen magazines, yearbooks, mascara, garter belts, letter jackets boys had given her to wear.

(What must that boy's family think, him going home with a girl his first break from Brandeis! Upsetting, too, that his name was "Antonio Vitarelli." Aunt Leonora let that slip out so everyone would be prepared, an Italian. With so many Jews at Brandeis, you didn't expect such a thing. But Elisabeth had always shown wisdom and logic in her choices, so one mustn't jump to conclusions.)

■ Thanksgiving, Elisabeth and Antonio Vitarelli were stationed at the front doorway, so everyone could meet him right away. He was entirely American, you could tell by his relaxed shoulders, the swing of his arms (so gorgeous in his nubby white sweater). "Please don't call me Tony," he said, manfully shaking Daddy's hand. "It just doesn't suit me."

"It's the same with me," Elisabeth added. "I could never be a Liz or a Betty." She gazed at Antonio as if it were this absence of nicknames that bound them together. Ruthie, suddenly shy, did not quite recognize Elisabeth, although there was no specific change in her appearance. She barely acknowledged Ruthie, and neither did anyone else, understandably; the aunts and uncles who usually fussed over Ruthie's grades and growth spurts now were buzzing about their Elisabeth, beautiful, more than ever, like a movie star, and look at him, what do you think, the Italian, such nice manners, even Elisabeth might lose her head over a boy who looked like that. (Eyes like that can make trouble for a girl.)

"Sure, he's a nice boy, why shouldn't he be a nice boy?" Leonora squared off against the curious multitude helping in her kitchen. "Elisabeth always has nice friends." But would a mere "friend" come home with her for a holiday? Didn't his own family want him?

Antonio and Elisabeth organized a hunt for marshmallow-roasting sticks for the younger children: Ruthie's brother Marvin and two small boys from a distant cousin they rarely saw. Ruthie hesitated to join this group because she was eleven, although she wanted to be with Elisabeth, and Antonio too, even though she felt strange around him. Soon they gathered in front of the fireplace, boxes of graham crackers and bars of chocolate nearby. She would have liked an invitation to Elisabeth's bedroom to hear about her new life, but there was no chance of that today.

"You want a stick—Ruthie?" He knew her name! Antonio was holding a stick out to her! She took it, growing warm as she got close to him. Somehow she couldn't look straight at him, as if she had forgotten how you look at someone, maybe because he was so tall. She didn't know what to say, the whole time letting her marshmallow char away in the fire while the little boys jabbered about Sky King and cowboys. Antonio and Elisabeth were laughing, encouraging the stupid talk about television while Ruthie couldn't think of a thing to say. Her face was burning, all of her was, maybe from facing the fireplace while she roasted her marshmallows. A few times she found herself watching him, the way his hair curled over his ears, the way he sucked some marshmallow off his fingers.

The entire activity was too exotic for the various aunts and uncles who had never been American scouts. So much dirt in the house, sticks and sticky fingers! Parents fussed at their children, warning them not to get too close to the fire, not to burn themselves.

Later, after stripping the turkey, which was undeniably dry, having absorbed the flavor of the paper bag in which it had been cooked, the dozen or so grown-ups gathered in the living room to assist Huntley-Brinkley with the news and to sample runny liqueur-filled chocolates. They compared what their doctors had to say about their sinuses, their digestive systems, their circulations. The little boys went outside to run around. Ruthie foraged for a deck of cards in Uncle Sol's study, ignoring his collection of stuffed birds, rabbits, squirrels, raccoons. He chose his specimens from roads and fields, already dead but not mutilated, and had them preserved precisely in their moment of death. Normally Ruthie preferred not to be alone in this room, but she needed a deck of cards so she could entice Elisabeth and Antonio into a game of 500 rummy, just the three of them.

But when she went to convey this invitation, it turned out that Elisabeth and Antonio were locked together in a corner of the dining room, kissing. Perhaps they were pretending that the slatted door opening out from the kitchen sheltered a private nook. Ruthie watched because she had never seen kissing like this before, this kissing entirely different from the pursed-lip pecks of her own experience, and also different from the loving but tired kisses that

Mommy and Daddy had, and still different from, but related to, long romantic movie kisses that involved a couple rotating their heads first one way and then the other. Neither Antonio's dark head nor Elisabeth's blond one swiveled at all. Antonio's jaw chugged up and down like a singing bullfrog's, as if he were drinking some needed substance from Elisabeth's mouth, and one of his hands spread across Elisabeth's head, fingers snarled in her gleaming hair. His other hand dug at the flat surface of Elisabeth's rear pocket as though he had lost something there. Though their heads barely moved, their mingled bodies, identically dressed (in white cabled sweaters and corduroy pants), rubbed and bubbled like boiling soup.

Ruthie watched for several minutes, holding her breath, sticky as if she were joined into this incredible activity herself. Then she tiptoed bravely past them, taking refuge in the kitchen, where she paced the dish-littered room without purpose. Soon Aunt Leonora came in, rattling a stack of cups and saucers. These she exchanged for a plateful of grapes, ignoring Ruthie.

Ruthie shadowed Leonora out of the kitchen. With alarm and even disgust, she saw the couple still cleaving and heaving in their well-lit, public corner.

"Now, now," clucked Leonora, pausing with the grapes. "That is enough, I should think."

The two heads stretched apart reluctantly, like taffy, leaving a sad, airless hole. Elisabeth turned toward her mother politely, but without recognition. Ruthie saw, as anyone behind Leonora would have seen, that her cousin's face had blurred, melted, the lovely eyes and lips and chin no longer defined but smeared and blended into flushed pink skin, while Antonio's face was pale and icelike, extruding manly black dots of beard, his chin deeply split, the wings of his nose rigidly hewn. Even his feathery eyelashes now jutted like spikes around eyes that earlier had resembled melting chocolate but now contracted into charcoal snowman eyes.

And Ruthie, sad hair furrowed by her plastic headband, stomach squeezed over the waistband of her plaid skirt (unevenly fastened with a decorative gold safety pin), fat legs weighted by collapsing kneesocks, Ruthie was choking on lumps of admiration and jealousy. That *was* jealousy finally, grabbing her by the throat and squeezing, as she would willingly have strangled her beautiful, dazed cousin had there been any chance she could have her place next to the boy, who was taking his time extricating his chest, his hand, his thigh from Elisabeth's. Meanwhile, Aunt Leonora lectured, "This isn't the place for that! Come now! What behavior! That's quite enough," as if she imagined that any of them were interested in her opinions.

It was clear to Ruthie that Leonora, short and square, had been squashed by the details of her life: bent by the weight of bad memories, the multitude of Thanksgiving guests and the complex menu, and her husband, Uncle Sol, who at any moment might forget where he was and fling himself into a closet, since his demons refused to leave him, preferring to hover nearby, waiting to overpower him. She was overburdened by her counters full of dirty dishes, and by the old relatives, who, lacking sufficient English, needed help negotiating their visas, their reparations, their rental agreements, their excursions to stores and to doctors. (Aunt Leonora shouldered these crushing tasks rather than her brother, Daddy, because she was capable with money and bureaucrats, understanding how to manipulate and negotiate to advantage, while Daddy's concerns were loftier: his lectures and papers, his research, his views of the state of the world.) She was crushed by her own difficulties seeing over the steering wheel when she drove, and even by the heavy grapes on the platter in her hands. Such loads rendered Leonora indifferent to Love, epic Love, Love which requires only that you take a step back and admire it from afar. Ruthie recognized Great Love from mythology, Renaissance paintings, and movies, but Leonora was unimpressed by True Passion, and kept pecking and clucking about their naïveté, their foolish idealism, their family backgrounds.

She informed the unhearing lovers that while Elisabeth came from fine people and most certainly Antonio came from fine people, too, no amount of smooching could change the fact that the two of them didn't belong together. Didn't they care that what they stood for, the very sight of them together, was repulsive, made her sick, and would surely sicken Antonio's parents, too? They were a slap in the face to all their fine people on both sides, especially those who were no longer living.

Briefly Ruthie saw those fine people appear in Aunt Leonora's dining room, rising from mausoleums and crypts and cemeteries and mass graves, lining up behind their respective offspring. Roman soldiers and buxom Caravaggio peasants with feet purple from stomping grapes, mustachioed barbers, opera singers, and painters painting ceilings while lying on their backs, pinstriped gangsters with machine guns, heavy dark women with mustaches and black dresses, robed monks with bald circles on their heads, nuns, and even a pope crowded behind Antonio Vitarelli, while behind Elisabeth the entourage contained wild-bearded prophets in sackcloth and ashes, men wearing wide fur hats and curled ear-locks, a king with a harp, doe-eyed girls with jugs balanced on their heads, women with kerchiefs and aprons swinging chickens by the feet, peddlers pushing clunky carts, bankers in spats and starched white collars, sharp-nosed women in furs, spectacled students carrying volumes of Spinoza, tanned pioneers in wire-rimmed glasses and kibbutz hats, and hollow-eyed wretches with shaved heads and yellow stars on their tattered striped uniforms.

The two mighty hordes pulled at their respective offspring, clawing them apart, so that even though Elisabeth and Antonio did return together to Brandeis University, it was evident to Ruthie that doom awaited them, as it did all Great Lovers.

■ On her winter break from Brandeis, Elisabeth spent the three weeks at home pining for handsome Antonio, who was with his own family in New Jersey. She wasn't herself at all, fighting with her parents over everything: she didn't wish to visit the relatives and wouldn't eat the foods Aunt Leonora prepared for her. She sat alone in her room, playing records, claiming she had no patience for her high school friends. She took long walks by herself, in the snow, without boots.

"Call her, Ruthie," Mommy ordered. "Ask her to spend an afternoon with you. Maybe it would make her feel good to spend time with a cousin near her own age."

Ruthie's hands shook as she dialed, aware of her presumptuousness—at eleven she was hardly Elisabeth's contemporary, even though Mommy always fantasized that they had a special relationship—and she stammered out the invitation, would Elisabeth take her to a movie or shopping.

"Really, Ruthie, you need to find some friends your own age!" Nastiness crackled into Ruthie's ear.

"I do! I have friends my age!"

"You can't sit around waiting for me to entertain you. If you have friends, you should call them."

"I have lots of friends!" Didn't she? As soon as she said it she had doubts. How dare she imagine Elisabeth would turn to a friendless creep like her? "I have plenty of friends to play with!" Probably her friends didn't really like her. Elisabeth's sigh wafted through the phone.

"I'm sorry, Ruthie. I don't feel very sociable. I wouldn't be good company."

"Oh." Ruthie tried to sound like she understood exactly.

"I miss Antonio so much. I didn't know being in love would be like this."

"Oh, sure."

"When we're apart I can't function, I'm not myself . . . I'm not anything!"

"It sounds awful!" said Ruthie, indignant that such love should be sundered, even temporarily.

"I've never been so happy in my life." Elisabeth's voice was weak, as if she were falling asleep. "Someday you'll understand."

But Ruthie was sure she understood already, thinking of Antonio, what it would feel like to be kissed the way he had kissed Elisabeth on Thanksgiving. Her lips would mash against her teeth, his cheeks would scratch her face. "Ruthie Ruthie Ruthie," he whispered, his eyes narrowing, seeing only her. She hugged herself, digging her fingers into her shoulders, shuddering with longing.

■ At the end of January, after failing to contact Elisabeth for five fretful days in a row, Aunt Leonora succumbed to a "strange feeling that something was wrong." She alerted Elisabeth's dorm housemother, who grilled Elisabeth's roommate, a tough New York girl who claimed ignorance of her roommate's whereabouts, remaining loyal to Elisabeth even though she knew all. The girl broke only when subjected to higher officials and intensified questioning, which in Ruthie's understanding had taken place in a soundproof room lit by one dangling lightbulb. The roommate, blindfolded and bound by bandannas that dug into her wrists and flattened her wiry New York hair, chewed her lips as burly professors in mortarboards sneered accusations at her: "Is it possible that there's been foul play? Isn't it a fact that you're an accomplice?" Finally, still refusing to speak, the terrified girl produced a wrinkled paper on which Elisabeth had scrawled, "We're off to Florida, ta-ta!"

It was that "ta-ta" which, to the family, signaled a rat—would a girl so serious, so sensitive, make light of such a grave situation? For her parents were certain that their only child, their miracle conceived and born in the ashes of a DP camp, had run off to marry *that Italian boy*. The family gathered, again at Sol and Leonora's house, but for what? A wedding? More like a tragedy!

■ "Be quiet!" Aunt Leonora greeted Ruthie's family at the door, her finger to her lips. "Sol is on the phone. With the FBI!"

"Can I see the puppy?" asked Marvin, who did not care that Elisabeth had ruined her life.

Ruthie's family tiptoed through the house, Mommy heading toward the kitchen with a bakery box while Marvin went to the basement to play with a puppy Sol and Leonora had recently acquired. You wouldn't expect Uncle Sol and Aunt Leonora to have a puppy. One of Sol's patients had given it to him, and Leonora thought it would make a nice diversion, a small consolation for Elisabeth's being so far away at Brandeis. But it wasn't much comfort. The puppy's yipping and yapping made Uncle Sol even crazier than usual, so they kept it locked in the basement where it cried all the time.

Daddy headed for the living room, with Ruthie right behind him. She did not immediately notice Tante Hilde knitting in a dark corner among the overstuffed furniture, despite the immense bulk overflowing the armchair. "A fine mess that brings us here, *nicht wahr?*" she greeted Daddy. Ruthie started to back out of the room. "Tell the child to bring me a glass of water," Tante Hilde said.

"GO, Ruthie," Daddy ordered.

Ruthie fled down the hall. The kitchen contained several other aunts, laying rolls and cold cuts out on trays. She opened the refrigerator to search for a bottle of seltzer, but Leonora pushed her aside.

"Ach, Ruthie. Why are you holding the refrigerator door open so long, spoiling all the food? Zena, why did you bring the children?"

The basement door opened a crack. At once a small beagle head lunged out, but Marvin grabbed it back and followed it into the basement.

"A family should be together at difficult times," Mommy answered, rolling her pretty eyes a bit. "And when in all the years did you ever leave Elisabeth at home?"

Leonora's round peach face twisted. "Elisabeth!" she moaned. "*Gott, mein Gott!*"

"Is there any news?" Mommy whispered in German. From the dining room one heard the thunderclap of Uncle Sol's voice.

"WHAT DO I CARE IF IT'S 'AFTER HOURS'! DO YOU KNOW THIS NAME: VITARELLI! SHE WAS TAKEN BY A VITARELLI! MAYBE MAFIA! DON'T YOU KNOW WHAT IS THE LAW!" Since he had spent the war changing papers, identities, hiding places, he was never entirely certain what year it was, what country he was in, what form of government prevailed.

"It's not so bad that he's an Italian." Leonora collected herself. Her fingers gleamed from touching cold cuts. "I just don't understand why they had to run away."

From the dining room: "I TELL YOU SHE IS TAKEN!" After all, he explained, Elisabeth, so beautiful, so accomplished, so reliable, his daughter—surely she wouldn't choose to disappear?

"You should sue the university is what you should do," said Aunt Cidi. "Then they'd find her quick."

On the stove, a pan of sausages ignited, shooting smoky flames to the ceiling. Women gasped and leaped out of the way: "Call the firemen!" Ruthie shrank back against the refrigerator, ready to throw Tante Hilde's glass of sloshing seltzer into the advancing inferno, but Leonora was already holding the pan under running water. Smoke and oily black rings floated upward. Squealing, scratching, and yipping came from inside the basement door. "Come back down here," Marvin's voice pleaded.

"Oh, that would have been a real disaster," Leonora said.

"Why are you fussing so much at a time like this?" Mommy scolded her sister-in-law. "Who will eat all this food, so much *braunschweiger,* so much *blutwurst?*"

"Everything will be fine," Leonora said. Only a few black spatters greased the wall over the sink. "We shouldn't get so excited." She took the dripping, charred sausages from the sink and lay them on a dishtowel. "I'll dry them off and they'll be just fine, good as new."

Ruthie headed for the living room with Tante Hilde's water, not particularly caring how cold it was. Women trooped ahead carrying trays, the meats, the cheeses, the cakes needed to pacify them this evening.

"You will hear from my congressman! He has met me!" Sol shouted. You could hear him crash the phone and the receiver together, like cymbals.

Tante Hilde took the glass without looking up at Ruthie's face. "Why did you take so long?" she scolded. "Every time I see you seem less capable. You are at that stupid age, I imagine." Ruthie had long ago learned not to respond to this great-aunt by breathing deeply and shutting her eyes. ("She means well," Daddy always said, as if Ruthie should acknowledge Hilde's goodwill.) The aunts were subdued, sampling chocolates, speaking of Elisabeth in the past tense as they comforted Leonora: she was always such a good girl, a boy would respect that; she still loved her parents, you could be sure, no matter where she was; many women survived youthful mistakes, sometimes they even turned out well . . .

A pale and wrinkled Uncle Sol settled on the sofa near Mommy. "I don't know . . . ," he sighed, pinching his nose. "They say in America things are different, but everywhere it's the same . . . a person disappears and no one lifts a finger . . . bureaucrats, criminals . . . " He began to shake—his entire family, taken: father, mother, brother, another brother, the two wives, all the children, babies, the youngest brother shot as they all looked on, no one left, no one left, no one . . . "Taken," he muttered.

"Stop this, Sol!" Leonora ordered. "Elisabeth wasn't taken away, she has run away! She will come back!"

"WHAT! RUN AWAY!" He stamped both his slippered feet under the coffee table so that the sausages trembled on their platters. "When they took my family, I run away! For years I run away! My daughter doesn't have to run away! She was TAKEN!" He began pacing the room, waving his arms and muttering.

This awkwardness didn't silence the room for long, because the family was accustomed to Sol's behavior. Daddy changed the subject.

"So how does a girl find an Italian at Brandeis University?"

"Italians are not good husbands," Tante Hilde declared, setting aside her needlework. "They drink and chase after other women as soon as they make the first child." She added that all winter long in Italy they shot migrating birds out of the sky. Bluebirds, larks, thrushes: no bird was too small for Italians to cook into their puddings and stews.

"Really!" Daddy said. "They shoot songbirds?"

She nodded her large gray head. "It is known." She had heard that so many were slaughtered during their winter migration over Italy that barely a bird remained to return to Germany in the spring.

Who could respond to that? There was no sound other than Sol's pacing and the clink of ice cubes.

"I wish I knew how to reach Elisabeth." Mommy refreshed her lipstick without a mirror. "I have a feeling she would confide in me. I haven't forgotten what it's like to be young."

"We followed all the advice about raising children: Dr. Spock, Ann Landers," Leonora fretted. "It's not like we kept her locked away." Her eyes puckered, real grief that made Ruthie want to cry, too.

"Still, she's afraid to talk to you." Mommy took a nail file out of her purse.

"A girl unmarried belongs with her parents!" Sol said, still moving, raking his sparse gray hair into alarming points.

"Such a beauty," Aunt Cidi added. "And she was smart about boys, wasn't she? She knew not to let them take advantages?"

"Great beauty can be a curse," Tante Hilde said. She was knitting again. "Perhaps in Elisabeth's case it has led to her downfall."

"Downfall!" Mommy snapped. "What a way to talk about your niece!"

"It's because she *is* my blood that I know. Some women can cleverly manipulate a man, but others are softer and easily fooled. Oh, I know very well what it is to be led astray by a man!"

Ruthie sat forward, wishing to hear just how Tante Hilde had come to be led astray. What man would have even dared toy with the woman buried fifty years into that hulk? She must have exacted terrible retribution. (But it had to be lies; if Ruthie never found a boyfriend, she thought she might tell such lies. She imagined herself old, headband scraping her sparse white hair away from jowls that wobbled as she told her bored descendants tales of ardent lovers and spurned suitors. If you told a lie often enough, it began to seem true . . . would she finally believe her own stories?)

From the kitchen a crash, splintering wood. A whiz of beagle flew into the living room, changing course every few seconds to avoid the densely packed furniture. Leonora rose from her chair, but though her square figure darted here and there, it never managed to occupy even the same quadrant of the room as the puppy. Marvin, running in pursuit, smashed against a curio cabinet, causing several teacups to spill onto the floor. Ruthie reached down and caught hold of surprisingly loose dog skin. She pulled the flailing puppy into her lap.

"Is nice doggy, no?" Sol observed as everyone caught their breath, straightening the results of chaos.

Ruthie lifted the puppy by its armpits and looked into the shaking spotted face. His eyes were deep and tragic, telling of early trauma: separation from his mother, random painful whacks on the nose, isolation in the basement.

"It's a good idea to have a watchdog," Leonora said.

"What does he watch locked in the basement?" asked Daddy.

"He must stay there until he becomes housebroken."

"My heart is broken!" Sol declared. Apparently the pacing potential of the living room was exhausted, for he opened the front door and strode outside, not bothering to take a coat or shut the door.

"Perhaps you should go to Boston," Mommy said, turning to Leonora and the business at hand. "You should talk to her friends. They will know more than anyone."

Leonora said she was considering it, and wondered if she could leave Sol alone in the house for a few days. At this, the puppy leaped from Ruthie's lap, pausing only to grab the string of blackened sausages, and catapulted against the storm door, which gave way.

"Marvin! Ruthie! Catch him!" Mommy ordered, but the two children were already after the animal, now a dark shadow running in ever-widening circles in the spotlit dirty snow. This startled Uncle Sol, who was also navigating the front lawn.

"Your coats! Your boots!" Mommy shouted. It was glorious,

the sting of snow melting into their shoes as they ran. The aunts bunched together by the door to watch the flailing, shouting, even joyful chase. Moments later, Uncle Sol leaped after the puppy. It veered, disappearing under the advancing headlights of a large dark car. The car slowed for a moment, during which all was quiet, then gunned its motor and sped away. The puppy lay in the road on its side, flattened, the string of sausages still clamped in its mouth.

"Oh, dear." Aunt Leonora wiped her mouth with her hand. "*Mein Gott.* Poor, poor thing." Marvin burst into tears and ran to the house, to Mommy. Ruthie didn't want to go in, but she was getting cold.

Someone said at least it was quick. Outside, Sol was heading toward the body—approaching the animal, she was certain, not as a grieving owner or even a doctor but as a collector, looking to augment that extensive taxidermy collection in his study. Leonora ran after him, her squat body quick in the cold, and pulled him away, back into the house.

Mommy was preparing to leave: it was late, the children were tired, so much excitement, they should not have come.

"The boy should not have let the animal out of the cellar," Tante Hilde observed. She had not gotten up from her corner, because she did not move easily. "A wild boy has no more sense than a wild animal."

It was true, Ruthie thought, shocked to find herself even partially agreeing with the mean old woman; even so, anyone could see that Marvin was terribly sorry, more than anyone else.

"It's not his fault," Daddy said, putting his coat on. "How could you blame Marvin? What happened was perfectly clear. I hate to say it, but this is the first time I have ever seen such a thing—an animal committing suicide."

■ Within two weeks of the dog's death, Elisabeth was returned home, transferred to Case Western Reserve, to lead a "quieter life and concentrate on her studies," according to Aunt Leonora.

As if Elisabeth had ever neglected her studies! Her life was a parade of awards and honors: besides being in the usual honor societies, she'd won a city-wide competition for her essay "President Kennedy: Changing America's Youth Forever," and a chapter of the VFW had chosen her as the first girl to receive the America's Best Hope award. For years already she had sipped coffee among the adults, crossing and recrossing her grown-up legs in their nylon stockings to explain precisely (pressing together the thumb and forefinger of her right hand) the flaws and dangers of the domino theory, the posturing of Madame Ngu. Naturally, she hadn't neglected her studies (hadn't Case Western accepted her at once, unconditionally, in the middle of the term?), and in the end it turned out she hadn't really "run off" with Antonio Vitarelli either. Rather, they had gone to a cottage his parents owned near Boca Raton, just for one week, because she greatly needed some sun. She explained this to Mommy with Ruthie right there in the room, but Aunt Leonora out of earshot.

Perhaps the escapade had been impulsive, Elisabeth allowed, lifting her beautiful, heavy-lidded blue eyes to punctuate her true telling of events. But she had been so tired just then, from all her classes, a pinching headache that never went away, and a scratchy throat more often than not. And Boston had been so cold that week, all fall really, cold and bleary except for Antonio, from her Principles of Psych class, who had loved her, whom she had loved. (And she made it seem reasonable that one couldn't survive under that kind of hardship, Bad Weather in Boston. Who else could get away with such melodrama: "From the beginning we were so close; so, so close," first willing and then holding back tears to puddle the blue, blue eyes that stared far away over Mommy's head. Her pink unpainted lips trembled as she spoke, so bravely it would break your heart to see it.) Antonio Vitarelli had suggested the vacation, just for the week; they could both easily make up their schoolwork, he was worried about her health and knew she needed rest, a week of hot sun . . . "And was it really so terrible that I went?" she asked them, her serene features a study in rationality. "I didn't mean to cause trouble. I really loved him. Could anyone have expected me to ask my parents?"

"No, not with their old-fashioned ideas." Mommy slandered her sister and brother-in-law while widening her eyes to show her comprehension of Elisabeth's grief. "Still, in the end you'll see your decision was good."

"Of course," Elisabeth agreed, one siren to another. "I have no regrets about anything, though."

"No, you shouldn't. There are always more men. You're entitled to adventures."

Ruthie sat quietly, hiding the excitement stirred by these womanly opinions, this affirmation of female wiles. She could feel Antonio's arms around her as if she had actually been in them . . . he was the most beautiful man she had ever met.

"I've realized how much I don't know," Elisabeth confided, and Mommy nodded: "You're wiser than you think."

She was studying psychology, seriously now, Aunt Leonora bragged; even though Elisabeth was only a freshman she was working closely with one of her professors who recognized her superior abilities, her seriousness . . .

"And she has read Freud?" asked an aunt. Leonora snorted. Freud! Of course Elisabeth had read Freud, long ago. To study psychology one read Freud, that was basic. Freud!

The aunt nodded, satisfied . . . if Elisabeth had read Freud she knew what she was doing, her commitment to the field was unquestionable . . .

In the library, the adult section, Ruthie looked for books by Freud. They were about sex, Ruthie thought; *Totem and Taboo* would be about forbidden things. Although, why "totem"? What could Freud have cared about Indians? And she had heard that Freud wrote about how girls wanted to have penises (you were allowed to say that word for scientific purposes if you didn't giggle or act silly), although she did not want one and could not recall ever having wanted one. She sat down to read one of the books, but despite the occasional word that titillated her interest (eros, phallus), she found her mind wandering away from the thick, incomprehensible words. She was certain it was not for this that Elisabeth had given up Antonio Vitarelli.

The Match (Blessed Is the Match)

In late September 1938, for reasons which have since been revealed, the German government expelled from its land all Jews holding Polish citizenship, some eighty thousand people (" . . . and it is important to remember," Daddy instructed his children, his voice trembling with outrage, "that most of these people had never set foot inside Poland, spoke not a word of Polish, and in fact acquired their unlucky papers after the Great War, through some scissors-mad treaty that shredded the old empires and patched Austrian and Russian provinces into Poland, but none of these places held any sentiment for people who had by then been living in Germany for years, without a thought for their birthplaces . . . "). On the appointed date, at four in the morning, security forces in black trucks swooped down upon their victims to carry out the expulsion orders (" . . . the coldest hour, long after the icy moon retires, and long before the faintest blink of sunrise," intoned Nona Brunhilde, even more Teutonically gloomy than usual. "No decent soul stirs at four in the morning, especially not that morning. Even the whores closed up shop; a few scattered crows cawed out their chilly nightmares, shuddered beneath oily feathers and huddled deeper in their nests; that night even the bats fled to their dung-heaped caves, because the blood of their prey had turned too cold for their vampirish tastes . . . "). The order excused no one who held a Polish passport, not one renowned professor, not one celebrated beauty, not one factory owner, not one popular singer, not one decorated war hero, not one dear friend of a judge, or a chief of police, or a mayor; no one was overlooked, not one toothless old woman, not one just-born infant, not one idle beggar, not one visiting cousin, not one locked-up madman, not one bedridden invalid.

Certainly not to be forgotten was Emmanuel Dubinsky, a real Pole, from Lodz, temporarily residing in the city of C—— while he completed his medical training, and also not his wife, and also not his two-year-old son, Rafael. ("That can't be right," said Daddy. "By 1938 the Jews had been thrown out of all the universities." "I don't know then," said Mommy, brushing his words away. "He was a doctor, from Poland, living in C—— with his family . . . who knows exactly why?")

"Dubinsky Emmanuel Dubinsky Eva Dubinsky Rafael!" called the brownshirts, knowing the names exactly. They battered the heavy oak door with fists cushioned by fine leather gloves, smashed the solid door with a determination that cracked the doorframe, with a hatred that caused the small chandelier just inside the door to vibrate and swing so that when, only seconds later, a terrified, sleep-ridden Emmanuel flung open the door, all the characters in the drama flickered and jerked as if they were in a silent movie: the three belted, booted, gloved, and hatted storm troopers screaming instructions; the one barefoot, uncombed, unshaven, pajama-clad doctor fumbling across his waist for the belt of his nonpresent bathrobe, whose pocket he fuzzily imagined might contain his glasses (the bathrobe, of course, was draped over a chair in his bedroom, near a nightstand upon which rested his gold-rimmed glasses, without which he couldn't quite comprehend the shrieks of the officials).

Even so, amidst the barrage of *"Schweinen!"* and *"Polen!"* and *"Juden!"* the message penetrated Emmanuel's muddled mind: as nationals of an enemy land they were to be returned to their homeland, at once! They must dress quickly and take only their passports, nothing else: no money, no possessions. He probably understood these orders immediately, even half-blind, swaying slightly, his bare feet cold on the wood floor, unmoving before these ghoulish figures that shouted at him to move (*"Schnell!"*), aware somehow that Eva, disheveled and shaking, lurked several yards behind him, half-hiding behind the bedroom door, clutching the half-asleep cherub Rafael, who whimpered and fussed more from his mother's tight grip than the shouting and banging in the hall. Emmanuel must have understood these shocking orders at once, because his first thoughts were how to circumvent them; not the deportation, which was incomprehensible, but the order to take nothing at all—! His mind raced over possibilities: to hide money on his person, on his wife's person, perhaps a bribe to these fiends . . . traveling with a small child, one needed certain supplies!

"Surely we can take a bag of essentials?" he asked, the first and only words he spoke to his captors.

"Take only your Polish passports!" To conclude the point, a club rammed into his shoulder, sending him stumbling toward the bedroom, where he and his wife numbly dressed, barely looking at each other as they piled on clothes, as many as possible, humiliated, not speaking because in their terror neither one had thoughts that they had words for. The only sensibility the Dubinskys felt was a fierce instinct to protect their child, and a vague supposition that, if they had a few minutes, if they could wake up, warm up, gain control of themselves, they would see that there was *something* they could do.

And as black trucks carted them away in the blackness, the inhabitants of neighboring apartments rolled over under their heavy down quilts, grateful that they might still catch another hour or two of sleep, sleep that would erase from their minds the existence of the pleasant but after all alien young family who had run afoul of the authorities . . . Too bad, reflected Frau Kreuzer, their landlady, who had occasionally cared for little Rafael, a sweet baby, she remembered sadly, turning her face toward the wall, beautiful black curls and so intelligent! A shame that these things had to happen! The way he had patiently stacked small wooden blocks one atop the next until they made a tower as tall as himself! And how he had laughed and clapped when they tumbled down! Reliable tenants, but troublemakers obviously, traitors of some sort. This created more work for her now: to scour the rooms in order to show them to prospective tenants . . . to remove the personal items . . . Eva's heavy silver candlesticks, remembered Frau Kreuzer, suddenly sitting up in her bed and adjusting her nightcap. A meter tall, with beautiful grapes and leaves swirling down the fine silver columns . . . just for safekeeping. The Hutschenreuther china she had always admired, service for twelve . . . if they ever came back. Her feet already scuffed the cold floor, seeking her slippers . . . a thick Oriental rug, waiting right next door. Better she than some scavengers!

All the deportees from C——— were brought to the ballroom of a hotel near the train station, some two thousand terrified people jammed into the room, huddled in miserable groups, crying children, panicked old women . . . but you know all this already, you've heard enough of such scenes.

Who knows what thoughts occupied these people? Some survived, of course, and tell us what they remember, but they can't tell any more precisely what filled their minds. In most cases, the thoughts were less lofty than we would like to believe: this one worried that the stove had been left on at home, that one fretted over a child's special doll that had been forgotten in their panic; one thought about how his possessions might be sent to him, another feared that her German boyfriend would never know what became of her; most wondered what awaited them in Poland, and all felt the throb of uncertainty in the pit of their stomachs, which nevertheless began to growl with hunger as the hours wore on.

During the short walk from the hotel to the railroad station, Emmanuel Dubinsky did not wonder about Poland, for he knew Poland and he loathed Poland, a primitive land where he had suffered constant slurs in every aspect of his life. "Your race is bidden, is it not," a professor, lecturing on blood transfusion, had publicly demanded, "to sanctify the Passover wafer with Christian blood?" ("Although Emmanuel must have been from a privileged family, well-educated and well-off, to have been accepted to the university, to become a doctor!") Carrying his sleeping child, with Eva at his side, stumbling in her soft high-heeled shoes along the picturesque cobblestones (the throng was herded through alleyways, to spare local traffic the disturbing spectacle of two thousand people being marched at gunpoint), his mind seethed against Poland, berating himself for not having gone to San Francisco, where he had an uncle. Once he had almost gone to the American consulate, but it had been raining, and Eva had problems with English. ("It makes no sense, when you think about it: I *am* but he *is*, right away you have trouble, today I *go*, but yesterday I *went!* It's so disorderly, many people can't stand it!") So now, herded through the alleys with dogs guarding the way, Emmanuel trembled at this new, entirely unforeseen turn of events and his evident inability to control even the most basic aspects of his life. His sleeping son jounced against his shoulder, weakened from a lifetime of slights, insults, and mistreatment, which resulted in his inertia, obsequiousness, and self-effacement, and his unshakable belief, despite massive evidence to the contrary, that in Germany he and his family could have a good life. ("Nonsense! What Jew, in 1938, still believed that a good life was possible in Germany?" "Well, a Polish Jew, evidently!")

And just before they reached the railroad station, delicate Eva fell to the ground, writhing and frothing, and of course not even Nazis could do anything about an epileptic fit, scream as they might—and people stepped back as much as they could, leaving Emmanuel to crouch down by his wife, to prevent her from striking her head on a stone, from swallowing garbage or rolling into shit. But first, saying either "Save, save" or "San Francisco," he handed the boy to Sol.

("Sol? Uncle Sol?" "Of course Uncle Sol! What did you think this was all about? Sol and Emmanuel had grown up together in Lodz, inseparable! They became doctors together, sought their fortunes in Germany together! Who would he give his son to but Sol?")

Sol, at this time, was a dashing figure, handsome, wealthy, unencumbered by family, and so well-connected that he had received advance warning of the expulsion and had eluded the security forces by spending that night in a convent! Still, after an agitated, sleepless night, Sol followed the trail of his fellow Jews, having first disguised himself in priestly garb, to be sure, and wanting somehow to help. In fact, even before sunrise, Sol, in cassock and collar, slipped in and out of the hotel ballroom as the unfortunate were processed, racing back to the homes of as many people as he could, retrieving for them medicines, jewelry, bankbooks, and other necessities that might alleviate some of their suffering. He did not find the Dubinskys in that throng, but later, when Eva fell to the ground, foaming at the mouth, Sol took little Rafael from his father's arms, so Emmanuel might attend to his stricken wife. Can you imagine Emmanuel's panic, the jostling crowd barely clearing a space in which his wife might convulse, the guards still and forever shrieking *"Schnell!"* Although they were too revolted by the seizure to remove Eva themselves, there was some danger that the schedule-obsessed Germans might force the crowd to trample the unfortunate woman. At that black moment, Emmanuel took no notice of his friend's strange costume, didn't even wonder at his sudden appearance, but naturally handed over the boy, even saying "Save, save!" in order to attend to his wife.

("He couldn't have been dressed as a priest! A priest wouldn't have been allowed into an area where Jews were being transported—the security was unbelievable!" "The way I heard it was *a priest*. Maybe he wasn't dressed as a priest then—maybe as a guard, maybe as a nun even. What difference? Remember, the unbelievable occurred every moment in those days!")

As he took Rafael, Sol was certain that Emmanuel said, "Moshe Dubinsky, San Francisco." So Sol disappeared with the boy, who after a few months was delivered to the uncle in San Francisco.

("But that's ridiculous! No one sent their children away in 1938! Later it was different, of course, but in 1938 people still imagined that they could protect their children!" "It's true, it's true, but the final truth is this: for some reason, Emmanuel Dubinsky, muttering 'San Francisco,' handed his son Rafael to his friend Sol, somehow disguised so he was not deported with the other Jews, and Rafael was, in fact, raised by the uncle in San Francisco, and not sent to Poland with his parents. Who knows if Emmanuel had actually intended for Sol to take the boy? And Eva, when she recovered, must have been frantic, insane with anger and terror, to discover her son missing! For as miserable as these people were, at that moment in 1938, they didn't begin to fathom that worse horrors awaited them. It is possible to imagine that Eva never spoke to Emmanuel again, never forgave him. There is no way to know what transpired between them as a result of Emmanuel's rash action, or perhaps it was Sol's impulsiveness; no way to know, for they were not heard from again. All that is known is that they were among the first sent to Auschwitz.")

And about Rafael, why, what is there to say? He did well in school, and played baseball, and the clarinet, and had a paper route, and led his high-school debate team, and played chess, and tennis, and excelled at the great Stanford University, where eventually he became a doctor of radiology, and in every way brightened the lives of his great-uncle and aunt. And some months ago Sol noticed the name "Dr. Rafael Dubinsky" in a medical journal, and made the connection, and contacted him, and invited him to visit. And two weeks ago, because of a conference at the Cleveland Clinic, he came, and that's how he met Elisabeth . . . and since then he hasn't been able to tear himself away.

■ Anna and Ruthie went to bed late, and still had so much to discuss, from their beds at right angles to each other, that they switched their heads and pillows to the connecting corner of their mattresses. "It's like a fairy tale, how they found each other," said Ruthie, pausing only a moment before betraying the fading memory of Antonio Vitarelli.

"You're so immature, Ruthie," Anna reminded her, cracking her own thirteen-year-old knuckles with authority. "It's not a fairy tale—this is real. Elisabeth is getting married to someone she's only known for two weeks! It's not like her; that's what's scary."

"But Mommy said—"

"Mommy just said she'd have a good life, but she doesn't care about if they love each other or have anything in common. It sounds like an arranged marriage, like in India or the Bible!"

Long after Anna became a shadowy mound, shrouded in blankets, Ruthie lay awake, assaulted by the confusion of dark images that was the story of Dr. Rafael Dubinsky, a two-year-old pulled from the trembling arms of his doomed father by Uncle Sol, who (perhaps disguised as a priest!) escaped deportation. Eighty thousand Jews herded to the trains, forced to walk through back alleys so as not to interfere with the morning traffic of Germans on their way to work. Packed into the dim, stinking cobblestone alleys so that decent people could avoid the stench of hordes of men and women and children and babies and graybeards and babushkas. ("There is a particular odor to a crowd of terrified people," Ruthie had heard once, when an adult had forgotten that she understood German. "Not what you'd expect, sweat or shit or any kind of organic body smell; it's something chemical, like sulfur or melting rubber.") Near the railroad station, Dr. Rafael's mother had fallen to the cobblestones, writhing and foaming among the horse droppings. Her husband, Emmanuel, handed his two-year-old son to Uncle Sol, and stooped down to help his wife, who was beyond help.

Once, when Ruthie was in third grade, a boy in her class, Peter Lee, had crashed out of his chair onto his back. "Stop that, Peter!" the teacher ordered, but Peter Lee could not stop it, body bridging and collapsing, hands flailing, chin bobbing and swinging in all directions; his classmates held their breath and stared, stared and looked away as a mound of creamy foam burst from Peter's lips, bubbled from between his clenched teeth, strings of foam sliding across first one cheek and then the other as his head jerked from side to side. The teacher ran to Peter Lee, brandishing a pencil, crying, "Open his mouth! Open his mouth!" although no one would have dared approach the disgusting figure; the third-graders only clutched the edges of their desks. The teacher stood over the jerking, frothing boy, holding the sharpened pencil in her upraised fist as if she meant to stab him through the heart, and just for a moment her own face convulsed, grimaced, and folded up as if she herself might fall to the floor. This facial contortion disappeared so quickly Ruthie thought she might have imagined it, although she knew she had not. The teacher ran to the ancient phone on the wall and shouted into it, "I need help in here! The Chinese boy is having a fit!" Then Ruthie understood, as the whole class understood, that this had something to do with Peter's folded eyelids and yellow skin, and that whatever was possessing Peter Lee could never touch them.

By the time the nurse arrived, screaming, "Everybody keep back!" everyone was glued in their seats. Debbie Minsky, whose desk was next to Peter's, whose feet could have reached out from her desk to step on the convulsing boy, had long ago slipped out of her own desk and squashed in with the girl who sat on her other side. "Everybody keep back!" But Peter Lee's feet had stopped their thrumming, and he lay heavy on the floor, his eyes blinking slowly. "All right now, all right now!" said the nurse, more to the class than to Peter, whose face she wiped with a towel before yanking him to his feet and walking him out of the room, her square nurse's hand clamped firmly to his limp shoulder. Peter Lee blinked and said "whu?" once. On the floor, where it happened, there were two puddles, a small one and a larger one, and everyone saw them and felt afraid.

"It's a disease in the brain," the teacher told the class, brushing at her bosom. "Because of some problem when he was born. He must have forgotten to take his medicine. An accident of birth."

■ Because of an accident of birth, Rafael Dubinsky's mother writhed and foamed in the crowded cobblestone alley, causing his father to hand him to Uncle Sol, and so Rafael was saved. Ruthie lay awake, considering the images that rose amidst the buzz of Mommy and Daddy in the living room.

"Because he happened to be born in Germany," Daddy's voice

suddenly boomed, "Rafael probably didn't *have* to be deported with his parents. They must have arranged to leave him with someone . . . possibly even Sol." And Ruthie heard the drone of Nona Brunhilde, risen from her lumpy bed in the tiny winterized porch off the kitchen, for Nona Brunhilde kept odd hours, rising or retiring for only two or three hours at a time, so that during the three months of the year that she lived with her son's family, it was necessary to whisper and tiptoe in the kitchen, to avoid creaking the cupboard doors or gushing the water faucet, while at any time during the night you might wake to shuffling footsteps in the hallway, or rumbling plumbing, or crackling from the enormous steeple-shaped radio that received stations from all over the world. Now Nona Brunhilde remarked in her droning German that the two sisters of her long-gone husband, two pioneers who had left Germany for Palestine in 1933, remained virgins *to this day* rather than marry Polish boys like Uncle Sol, which were all that were available in that primitive place. . . . "Sol's hardly a Pole, trained in Germany and married twenty years to *your* daughter!" Daddy shouted at his mother. "Who cares about these things anymore!"

"It always shows up somehow," intoned Nona Brunhilde. "Leonora's Pole is a madman." This new description of Uncle Sol made Ruthie giggle into her pillow, muffling the squeak and clank from the medicine cabinet that was Daddy getting his headache pills.

"The truth is, they're treating that poor girl as if they were still in Lodz," Mommy's voice said. "Marrying her off like that. Poor child. Forcing her into an arranged marriage. Like a hundred years ago. Like Indians. Like Arabs."

And in the dark over Ruthie's bed loomed Elisabeth, chains dripping from her wrists and ankles, beautiful in a harem costume with her stomach exposed, her blond hair bound in a turban, her mouth slack and even drooling as Uncle Sol pulled a long, brilliant anesthetizing needle from her arm, while nearby a man, also turbaned but visibly Polish in a white peasant shirt and knee boots, a goatee curled to a diabolical point, proffered a pirate's chest of gold coins and jewels and dishes and tablecloths and medical diplomas to Aunt Leonora, whose squat little figure danced in its dark housedress.

■ On Tuesday evening, Uncle Sol and Aunt Leonora invited all the family to their house to present Dr. Rafael Dubinsky, their almost son-in-law, who as an infant had been saved from Hitler's ovens, saved by Fate (with dramatic assistance by Uncle Sol), and swept halfway around the world to find his destiny with their only child Elisabeth, another miracle, born under an American flag at least, but still in Bergen-Belsen, still among ashes, although by then it had become a DP camp.

"It is the most beautiful story I have ever heard," Ruthie told herself Tuesday morning, and during lunch period at the music academy she told it to the other three sixth-grade girls. They were not her friends exactly, not like her true friends Paula and Jane and Maggie from public school (barely two months after Mr. Klankert told Mommy there was no place in his school for someone like Ruthie, she hardly saw them anymore, not even her best friend Paula, who had shared with Ruthie a hatred of fractions and an artistic, mature love for John Lennon, even though all the other girls preferred the superficial cuteness of Paul or the silly posturing of Ringo). But in the tiny music academy there were only four sixth-grade girls, too few to form alliances and divisions; they were stuck with each other. "You have your music in common, don't you?" Mommy had said, urging her to invite her new friends over. "Art is a mighty bridge."

But art didn't span the gap between Ruthie and the Bible-quoting harpist Mary Kate, a girl whose hair and skin and eyes appeared as colorless as the wax floating in the glass *yahrzeit* candle jars that frequently sat on the Kimmelmans' kitchen counter in memory of dead relatives. Mary Kate dripped crosses and dangled loaves and fishes. When Mary Kate stroked and plucked her harpstrings, it seemed as if she were rehearsing for her place in Heaven.

"Art is a mighty bridge," claimed Mommy, but art could not bridge the chasm between Ruthie and bony, silent Delia, a ghost lost behind a veil of hair and thick glasses. Delia floated through the halls of the music academy as if she were in a bubble, with one hand gripping her violin case and the other holding an open book before her face. "What are you reading?" Ruthie had once asked her. This invasion had caused Delia to turn white and sink her chin into her chest before scuttling away.

And art spun only the thinnest filament between Ruthie and black-eyed Satsuki, crackling with genius, who played her flute with a local chamber orchestra and had had a solo debut in Switzerland. She was excused from the detested music theory class, where Ruthie struggled among the nonprodigies, some only seven years old. Satsuki used these hours to refine her technique, as her mother and her flute teacher hovered nearby, plotting her next strategic move.

These three sat with Ruthie around a square wooden table in the red velvet, sconce-lit cafeteria of the music academy. "I'd like to tell you the most beautiful story I've ever heard," Ruthie began, turning red with importance and good feelings, and words rushed out of her, a torrent of relatives and Nazis and miraculous coincidences swirling around her as if she herself were at the center of the events. The other three girls unwrapped sandwiches, chomped into apples, sipped waxy milk through soggy straws as Ruthie orated the history resulting in her cousin Elisabeth's betrothal to Dr. Rafael Dubinsky.

"All the good Germans slept undisturbed while the Jews were being expelled," Ruthie explained, quoting precisely from the jumble of accounts she had heard and overheard during the past forty-eight hours. Delia, the mute violinist, licked jelly off her fingers and then lowered her head to retreat behind her messy curtain of hair, fingering her ever-present book. Ruthie, unable to stop, unfolded horror after horror until she revealed the worst: "And his parents were among the first sent to the gas chambers."

Mary Kate blinked her watery eyes and stretched her thin bluish fingers before her as if she expected a harp to appear from the chandeliered ceiling. "'He works judgment upon the nations,'" she recited, fingers twitching, "'heaping up bodies, crushing heads far and wide.' Psalm 110."

This gloomy recitation stopped the flow of Ruthie's story. "He works judgment . . . "—as if the Jews deserved to be killed, a thought that wafted like a bad smell over the table in the dim cafeteria, which was quiet but for the hum of conversing musicians and the occasional percussion of clinking forks and rattling coffee cups.

"You mean Hitler," Ruthie said, face heating as she prepared to defend. "You mean Hitler heaped up the bodies." She puffed her cheeks at Mary Kate, trying to look fearsome.

"No, no," trilled Mary Kate. "Hitler wasn't in the Bible." She sat very still, waggling only her lower jaw, like a marionette. "Some people see the devil everywhere, but that psalm is about God helping King David kill his enemies. Another psalm I know goes like this: 'Fair Babylon, you predator, / a blessing on him who seizes your babies, / and dashes them against the rocks.' Don't you think that sounds like Hitler, too? But it means that revenge is fair, Ruthie." Mary Kate spoke wisely, a waxy and transparent witch, angering Ruthie with her babble of smashed heads, of dashed babies, her Hitler and Babylon. What right had Mary Kate to these images? "I have memorized eighty-five psalms so far," Mary Kate said, folding her hands before her.

If only she could finish her story, Ruthie thought. She needed to tell her beautiful story. She began again, detailing Elisabeth's many sad loves and Dr. Rafael Dubinsky's prodigiousness. "And now he's a world-famous radiologist," she exaggerated.

"Fame isn't everything," said Satsuki, stroking her glossy black hair. "When you're famous, people may not love you when they say they do. They might be in love with your fame. This is why your cousin wants to marry this man after only knowing him a few days." She bobbed her head, sure of her own truths. "I will only marry someone as famous as I am."

It seemed to Ruthie that she was encased in an airtight glass box, suffocating with all that she knew, and that each of the other girls around the table sat in her own glass box, surrounded by her own absolute truth; and though the girls gestured and made faces at each other, no meaningful sounds or ideas could pass among the sealed glass cages.

She ripped open her own lunch bag, untouched until now, sorry that she had dared to tell this story to these outsiders. "Two cousins of mine got married after they met for the first time at the wedding of another cousin," Mary Kate was saying. "They had a baby that died, for punishment. That's just like what happened to your cousin, isn't it, Ruthie?"

Ruthie didn't answer. She had revealed a flower growing from a dungheap, and the girls wanted to trample it. "Save, save," she told herself. After a few minutes the girls talked about something else.

■ Because Mommy had changed her outfit so many times, the Kimmelmans had to park two blocks away from Uncle Sol and Aunt Leonora's house. Cars were parked on both sides of the quiet street, with no regard for regulations. Some pointed north and some south, and some tilted lopsided with two wheels up on the parkway as if they had been abandoned in a hurry.

"My God," Mommy kept saying as they hurried past hedges, iron fences, mirrored balls on pedestals. "My God. Selling their daughter. That poor girl. In this day and age. Like in the shtetl." Her heels rattled the sidewalk like castanets as she led the procession of Kimmelmans to her sister-in-law's large brick house, thrusting her chin so far before her that the wound coil of red hair faced behind her, looking to Ruthie like a bird's nest that had spilled all its eggs.

"Calm down, Zena," Daddy kept saying, a step behind. "Wait until you've met him, at least." Which caused Mommy to stop in her tracks, grind her fists, and say, "I don't know why I'm here, after the way I'm being treated." For after failing for two days to arrange a preview visit from her dearest niece and the miraculous fiancé Dr. Rafael, Mommy decided this match was brought about through deception, coercion, and foul play. "I just want to get to know him a little," Mommy had cajoled, bending into the phone, first to Elisabeth herself and then to Leonora. "If not for dinner, then for coffee. Half an hour. Just so I can form an impression. Suddenly she doesn't have half an hour for her aunt and uncle?"

"They've got no time, with the wedding so soon," Leonora insisted. "You'll meet him Tuesday night, at our house, with the rest of the family."

Something's wrong, Mommy had decided, swearing she wouldn't go Tuesday night, even as she scheduled an extra appointment with her hairdresser. It's a forced marriage, she said, they're tricking that little girl into a wedding with some disgusting old goat and in two months she'll wake up and wonder what happened to her.

Trees and houses blurred past as Ruthie and Anna trailed in the wake of Nona Brunhilde's medicinal cologne, profusely applied in place of the American custom of daily bathing, which wore away the body's natural disease protectors. Suddenly Anna stopped and bent over, sliding her hands over her skinny shins, smoothing nonexistent wrinkles out of the stockings she got to wear because she was thirteen. "I hate these things," she told her sister, although her self-satisfied smile, awash in lip gloss, belied her words. Hours ago Ruthie had dreamed that Elisabeth might ask her to be a bridesmaid, but the white socks sagging and flopping around her own ankles suggested to her that these aspirations were in vain. Anna took off, tugging at her garter belt through her skirt, Ruthie slogging behind as if her waistband were about to break and her shoes might fall off. So many cars, pointing the way to her cousin's house! Bringing so many cousins, old friends from the cheerleading squad, sorority sisters, bridesmaid material whose hair flipped up without ever using a roller and who were old enough to wear lipstick. Who were all these people, anyhow, when Mommy had said just family would be here?

Why would a beautiful nineteen-year-old girl like Elisabeth even think about getting married in this day and age, Mommy's voice rattled on, as if she had never said marrying a doctor was the best thing that could happen to a girl, especially one who had already "experienced life," which Elisabeth had most certainly done with Antonio Vitarelli when they ran away to Florida. Those things happened certainly, it was not the end of the world, but when a girl got slightly brown around the edges it was best to make salad quickly. Otherwise, a girl could wilt entirely, turning limp and black and putrid like Mommy's friend Manya Turkle-taub, whose skirts got tighter and necklines got lower and lipstick got redder each year that no man married her.

"She's throwing her brains away. And why the rush? What does *that* look like?"

"Calm down," Daddy was saying as they crowded onto his sister's front porch, which overlooked the remains of last week's tulips. Marvin, the youngest, got to ring the doorbell, while Ruthie was mashed into the hard molded bosom of her grandmother, who clutched a mysterious, badly wrapped package in her hand. A buzzing inside the house seemed to press outward against the bricks, growing louder by several decibels as the heavy carved door opened to reveal square-shaped Aunt Leonora in front of a bubbling mass of bodies. Ruthie remembered Daddy saying that in noisy crowd scenes, actors were told to say "rhubarb, rhubarb, rhubarb" instead of meaningful words.

"Ahhhhhh!" called Leonora, raising her arms high like an opera singer. "Here you are! Here you are!" And Mommy abruptly terminated her harangue and showed a happy face full of teeth to her sister-in-law. "We-e-e-e-elllll!" Mommy squealed, triumphantly lifting her own arms with such vehemence that her piled crown of hair appeared to grow taller. The arm waving and shrieking did nothing to alleviate the congestion on the packed doorstep, and as neither Mommy nor Aunt Leonora took a step toward each other, Nona Brunhilde gave a mighty heave, which sent Ruthie stumbling into little brother Marvin, and then they were all inside, the Kimmelmans added to the swarms of aunts and uncles of varying distance and degree who had come to meet Dr. Rafael Dubinsky, the son of Uncle Sol's boyhood friend from Lodz, Dr. Emmanuel Dubinsky, who had perished in Auschwitz, but not before getting his two-year-old Rafael to relatives in California, in order that the boy could grow up to become a radiologist and marry Uncle Sol's beautiful daughter Elisabeth, a small revenge against Hitler's infamy.

Block Bébé

Each night, steam-bright, a cooling slice of moon dangles from
    my doortop.
For seconds I believe I'm dreaming the white-blue flare, the
    shuddering
ash stub, my uncle's legs.

This dream a life. Blankets frame my breasts
as I float awake to a lamplit face
against the jamb. Tugging

my baby's hand, my lover escorts her for her goodnight kiss,
    his cough
inquiring when and if
I'm ready.

I'm never when he's in me, caught
in the mesh of my daughter's howls, imagining—
moving with him—her fists beating crib slats,

eyes hellish with weeping when I shift suddenly loose,
steal breath and space until, freed,
the stinging arc of my ribs

releases. Then, in my mouth, the silt and grit
of memory, pungent as an orange. Tasteless
as the blahblahblah of days, and again I'm the block bébé

in Rousseau's primitive painting, my wooden infant face
mottled ivory-pink, paralyzed with rage as, "pour fêter" only,

I dangle my marionette uncle from his strings, his
    upside-down heat

irradiant in every pore of his after-shaven face when he presses,
slowly as he dares, the still-flaring cigar between my left foot's
middle toes.

All that memory or dream. I have a lover, I tell myself now.
I desire a lover inside me, yes,
the sweat-heat of love parting my lips

though I rise, suddenly, so violently I'm aware, wrap my breasts
in their burn-hole robe, hoist my sobbing daughter. Mornings,
    straddling
her rocking horse, for minutes

she chews the mane. Watching her, I pray.
Or pretend we're some woman Rousseau never painted, a woman
washing dishes, her apron a pink frill in her lovely, sunlit kitchen

as she pulls strings of caked chili and onions
from the pan, slides them into her mouth, their webs separating
without giving her pleasure, texture, or taste as she gazes,
    through the window,

at her daughter in the sandbox,
pictures her daughter dead and files another nail
on her shapely, wooden hands.

Puppets

When only we're left to hear, you firk another quarter
from your jeans, induce Jack's fit on the first day of our
   honeymoon,
your semen between my thighs as I watch the puppet
crank up to laugh and dream of lying against your chest
beneath the high yellow arc streetlamps cast
on a steamed car window. Here stands Musée Méchanique

with its baby-sized puppets, hand-cranked, Lilliputian farms—
dozens of tiny farm folk, darkies grinning and shimmying
for a quarter; and jolly Jolly Jack, whose laugh
roars through the room, whose head lolls, pink lips tremble
with hidden saliva, black
plastic hair a Vitalis-hard slickness.

When he shakes and shudders, the laugh filthy as a sailor's
trading cunt jokes with buddies, the whole room
gets confused, gazes flash to the dirty wood floor.
Jack's arms shake in a tight
but widening arc as if cupping a dance partner's
expanding waist. Leaning against your green sweater

redolent of salt and wine, I don't know why I'm drawn
to grotesqueness any more than I knew why, as a child,
I could never look at the one-armed man who served corn dogs
in a dusty green café near my grandmother's house. That man
was so kind. Tongue-tied, a folded *Archie* crinkling my palm,
I didn't dare look for fear I would cry as he wrapped

greasy, breaded corn dogs in waxed paper, thrust them
tenderly into the bag that already held two hamburgers
with onions for my grandmother, kept up flirtatious patter
that turned her the shade of a dying tulip

as we glanced at each other bashfully
because we couldn't figure out where to leave our eyes.

One of his pressed white shirt sleeves was empty, hung from
    his shoulder
like a tiny, deflated ghost, and, though I told myself it was vile
to look, how could I stop? There was something almost lovely
in its particularity: the immaculate sleeve
with tiny, intricate stitches crisscrossing to the shoulder;
the starched outer seam; and beneath it, nothing,

as if he'd clothed air, though what I desperately wanted
was to peek inside that shirt and see what he *really* looked like,
just as, sometimes in the bath, touching my own lengthening
    breasts,
I wondered if all girls looked like me, the thought burgeoning,
from pilfered *Playboy*s, that perhaps they didn't, and that,
that was terrifying. After he passed us our goody bag,

my grandmother and I retired to a wooden picnic bench outside,
his small, round head framed in the smeared glass window
that looked out from the café, as, neck and shoulders jerking,
he chopped onions while we ate, the breading coating my tongue
    with crumbs
as I bit down into the dog because I was afraid I'd cry
from the horror and wonder of that empty sleeve.

Jack's rumbles subside and I squeeze your hand to urge "Stop"
when you slip another quarter in. We're alone now in the Musée
because who besides a masochist could endure, for minutes,
    the bray
rattling through floorboards to nerve endings in our feet?
You *must* be a masochist, I think, because you married me
and I'm afraid of so many things: entropy, an exploding sun,

rips in the ozone, the impaired turning less perfect
all the time. You grip my shoulders as Jack revs up
like a prizefighter for the KO, but he's only laughing,
his chest expanding, contracting with orgasmic mirth,

and I see, behind him, a tiny framed picture of Mrs. Jack,
a fat, ugly puppet in a sprigged red dress, cheeks ruddily
    inflamed

but blue eyes sad, and I lean back into your arms and remember
how you entered me only an hour ago, something restorative
about lovemaking when we're half-asleep and rectangles of
    dawnlight
lie soft and gray and powdery on sheets, and I was so wet
you pushed in right away, and though I might have been ugly
    minutes before
I was perfect again and not Jolly Jack's wife with her glass-eyed
    futility

that chills me as she cowers behind an explosive laugh.
As Jack shudders and stills, I press my mouth
into the sweet green grittiness of your sweater, think of
the man who sold corn dogs peering out onto a dusty, narrow,
small-town street, not caring about cracked panes, masking
along the serve window's sides; and remember, suddenly, the
    paraplegic

who sells African violets for two bucks from a wheelchair cart
he motors through traffic every day of his life, up and down
steep San Francisco hills; a man who's never been hit
but would be amazed if it happened because he feels in control,
whatever's explosive and ugly and damaged in his life
subsumed by those moments he rests in his chair

on a sidewalk, sun slanting under the back-tilted brim
of his Giants cap, and people, one by one, remove
potted violets, drop eight quarters into the jar on his cart
or, if they don't have change, two dirty, crumpled bills.

Three Marys

In the blackening light that dapple of blemishes
on their backs made her want them. And, rose-gray or red,
how easily she tipped them to their glistening pale underbellies
silvered with moon. A "huddler," they called her—a Mary
   who loved
rocking, awaiting any toad that eyed her bulbous-mouthed
then sank. All three Marys huddled. In their sixth-grade
   homeroom
the redheaded Mary shrank from stark noonlight as though she
were a bloodsucker. The blond Mary, a giggler, snorted over
   Classic
Comics while, in her skull, reflections roiled of her breast-budding,
mirrored torso. Brunette Mary, the "Anguisher," dreamed
noon and night of animals. In the silence of her soiled kitchen
she felt herself flush from socks to undershirt as if
boiling out of her body to gaze down at her momma's parted
hair, forced to swim farther and farther out
from the boozy table glass to see her own dwarfed body cradle,
   stroke,
a rubbed-velvet doe muzzle or wonderfully hefty toad.

It was their eyes she kept craving. Mauve and bubble-soft.
In art class her watercolors only soiled clean paper.
Where have you been, her mother demanded
when, that Thursday, October 27th, she materialized at the screen
in her fuchsia sweater and jacket, cupping a sealed jar.
Mary didn't answer. She'd left, she knew, her friends on their beds,
each stiffening with a sorrow she could scarcely describe
to the gaunt coveralled woman whose red-rimmed eyes
swam a little sauced. The clock chirped out its cuckoocall angst
as Mary carried the jar to her room. Inside, a fat-bellied garden
spider struggled to attach her web. Tossed her silk everywhere.
But the slick-glassed jar sides furnished no twigs. Mouth pressed

to her palms, on her bed Mary watched the spider circle faster
and faster. No fly to catch her. In that glass, alone,

the three Marys crouched. Passing her hand
through topsoil and moss, seeking halved squirrel-shells nutmeat
had abandoned, Mary the Giggler, bored
with the game, proposed another to that darkening silence.
To take off their clothes. To stand naked under starshine's
tentative glow. To reveal
their scars. Mary the Giggler removed
her plaid jacket. Brunette Mary noticed with quickening
interest how Mary Giggler's breasts puffed up
her T-shirt. Red Mary sheared
the dead foliage off a branch,
stabbed it into the dirt till it broke. Dusk
broke then, flinging its violet gauze, slightly startling, over Mary
Giggler's body as she peeled off her black T and stepped out of
her underpants. Red Mary glanced. The freckled moon
of her face stole white glow from those legs,
her mouth moved left and right as she circled with Brunette Mary
the trunk of Mary Giggler's body, the paling slash where she'd
driven her left knee into a barbed-wire mesh, the long twist
back of her calf where Mary had fallen on broken glass and torn
herself open on the street.

Then—Red Mary's turn. That's what Brunette Mary recalled
though, on her bed, the spider discombobulated
in her unfurnished jar, she could scarcely remember
dusk deepening then or how the whitish tree trunks sank outlined
to shadow. Red Mary, trembling, circled a sagging oak.
The clothes that she dropped on one tree side blossomed holes.
A ripped, filmy undershirt, pinkish shredded
panties. Brunette Mary pictured herself outside
her body, her lips swallowing blackness as they rounded
their o's. Red Mary sidled. It was a velvet-black
evening, and her body shone lovely as a planet, a star, as she
    floated
into their midst. Brunette Mary gazed up that V to her breasts
at the extraordinary crimson of Red Mary's body. Crisscrossed

with scars
lacing and looping, like paint splashes they blotched or ran,
some ragged where the wounds were still fresh, some scabbing
    over,
frayed and crusty, others half-pried as if Mary
had picked them. And beyond that, the starkness of Red Mary's
    white
body, the translucence of what must have been her skin beneath
wounds, the thick-throated hoarseness of the toads
near the banks, their gusty bellowing shifting distant and closer,
closer and away, as the three Marys, in a tightening cluster just
beginning to shiver, listened and listened.

The Meatpacker's Dream

begins with the redness. The smell of something sweet
boiling in the vats. The scalded hides,
loops of eviscera swept into piles

on a floor slick enough to slide on in steel-toed rubber boots.
Begins with a sunburst of veins, bleeding eyes, matted fur,
mouths glistening, grunting, bleating, mewling,

fat tongues lapping—
What if I lie here, night after night, fetus-tight while you push,
blunting the cut of our silence with no after never *yes?*

Begins, when you're in me, with the first animal that lies down in
    the road.
To build is to dwell.
The carcass is a house, I want to cry:

as I crouch, my view is shadows
shifting and bluing in the black-light meld covering a wheat field,
obliterating a town

which now lies sleeping, all the smooth pale faces
a blandness I summon each A.M. I lace my boots, tie my apron,
the air a pungency of white, cold, odorless dawn.

I sit in the field, stubble slicing me.
I lie down to watch
though only fluted ears are visible above stalks

so I rise, finally, for the black ribbon insinuating itself
around the slashed throat, the rotting hump
moon-bleached while I hold myself rigid as still shots in a dream,

black-and-white ecstasy, your teeth nibbling

neck and nipples and stomach and thighs as I
bend over the bone pile that crumbles, compresses, stains

into a grease spot darker than the rest of the rutted road and
the heart
in its lingering softness, pallor, and heft.

Skulls in the Woods

Light was the lure. It seared violet into my veins
    until I craved clouds that would swallow me
        like bath steam, pale and translucent.

Amorphous, my breasts swam a pink baby
    sweater that day the bad boys told me what
        they'd found, that day, rippling with light-

longing, I penetrated the forest, strolled by a stream
    coursing white toward a site with crushed branches
        where the forest folded over into deepening shade.

Crusted, black where the brain had rotted out,
    the skull had cracked to a ferment of thought and lost
        soul, that woman

winging in cold air pockets under treetops though they didn't
    know who she was or even if she was murdered. . . .
        I didn't scream. Crouched

over the loamy dirt floor where it lay,
    a spider web-threading the mud-blackened eyehole.
        Don't touch, my mother had said.

To touch took only a minute, the bone so fragile I could've
    crushed it. Behind the forest's laced
        green walls

traffic roared. I glimpsed, through the foliage, a few
    speeding trucks, their silvered sides
        lightning, and I held the skull close

to examine it, I clutched it as if protecting it, hating

those boys, hating the men and trucks and rocks and streams
and trees that had duped her, her black eyeholes lit with

the glints I lifted her toward, the smell of my new breasts
everywhere, the rich, hot gush
of my own mama's milk in my mouth,

in my mouth that never cried. A reclusive child, they said,
given to fits of moroseness, brown studies
where I'd hunch for hours in the bath,

fingers wizening. I never told a soul. That day I discovered
the skull Mama's wooden spoon beat the batter
to a frenzy, in my mind a forest blossomed

and blackened from one silly season to the next, the skull
dust-cracked then glistened as rain drove its stains
deeper into bone until its ugliness was genetic.

I cupped the skull to my breasts, tamped
and smoothed over its dirt nest with saddle shoes
until, it seemed, the whole forest floor was stroked

to mirror, until even my skin gleamed as I licked
the spoon, the batter clumping in my mouth,
my hyperactive brother vaulting up- and downstairs

while the rest of my family huddled in their TV circle. . . .
The skulls were there. Thousands
of them, I knew, planted behind stones,

under the emerald-green waterfall toward the center
of the forest, where it was so silent not even
a bluejay called, and I lived

in that vacuum, in the quiet of skulls
those boys had bestowed, with lewd winks and nods, once
and for all time, my grandparents aglow

when moon poured through leaves to ignite them
     like lighthouses, their glossy eyes watchful
          when I summoned their souls

to my bed, preparing, at twelve, for a life my family
     would never know, the beauty of one ugly skull
          streaming out through my tears and through all

my breathing pores.

The Sexual Jackson Pollock

I want him in me.

Don't tell me he's dead. Wild, drunk,
he could dance on smashed bottles, not slash
a toe. I burn for him as he burned tilting

the bottle in a heated chug
then tossing it to paint.
Mysticism, ecstasy, the bile-green's undercoat

a swash of pure black: words, words, words.
Paint's the thing. The rich, rhythmic slide
through veins drained of blood. The heart

stripped to brittleness and ache,
the job that deadens, the devouring, cowering
family, all, all, all

redeemed. Bucket-toss, slipper-soled ballet-glide.
Deft cowboy shuffle.
Struck whiter than butcher paper

he prances. Oh, he dances: his paint,
his pain, that love
in our veins
stains heart tissue

black, darkens us
like memory.

2

I want him
in me. On the ceiling
paint lariats twirl
and dim. In my
bedroom washed gold
with car beams I lie
blinded, the light's
dimming sadness like
paint I splatter, like
blood. In my room, arctic
cold: someone steps
on Jackson's grave.
Maybe, guilt-ridden,
another day
he'll skirt the bald
brown plot like cracked
glass so no cries
shove up like shards
through his soul. Through
their glass-studded slippers
my feet dripped blood as I
approached the body, the
onlookers fluttering
with flat, choral cries
when I crouched, kissed
one arm flung back
over his head then tugged
it straight, at peace with
the other. As his film
snippet plays my ceiling
again, in a Dick-and-Jane
mumble Pollock invokes
the holiness of paint, grit
and grain of spirit as a
drenched brush ascends
with a ghostly
high beam's sweep, as a

black-and-gray
Jackson leaps on both feet
propelling him up patterned
tiles, the brush
humming in its blackish glow
then tilting, tilting,
splattering the ground-laid
canvas with beautiful
precision, paint arcing in
long, black, choreographable
streaks. Thirteen, wild
with love, I wanted
to cup his bare feet,
create a Pietà with the
cowboy artist splayed
across my lap, his
face wiped clean of death
like the Magic
Marker slate children peel
to erase. I'd forgotten
how I loved them. How
I dreamed of caressing
those feet as if I could
lure Pollock's broken
body down from sky, the
face blasted bloody from
tree bark and glass, the
body an object I twist,
to and fro, in my two
trembling hands, testing
it for breath, for
movement, for strength,
stroking his long,
twisted feet as they float
from my grasp, as the
stretcher ascends toward
silence or perfect
pain, as the white doors shut
on our separation dance.

The Winter Barrel

I remember how everybody seemed to be flowing toward the light coming from a barrel of fire guarded by brown men. The flames peaked for snatches of air. All around were wild children, brown crates and garbage, brown patches of snow and brown mud glistening in the cold. I watched LaNell stand alone as the wild girls passed around her and formed a loose moving gauntlet down the rest of the paved block toward the vacant lot off West Madison with its flame-licked barrel and dazed men.

The tide of battle rose so swiftly, neither the men of the barrel nor the women in the walk-up windows could intervene. But I learned that was the flow of things. I just watched LaNell from the top of the school steps. She looked like a fawn with eyes hard and dark as coals, her lips twisted with annoyance. The first phase of the harassment had mugged the softness from her face. I understood. My innocence, my softness had fallen about the same time as hers—within a week after I arrived from Alabama, the wild children had started in on me, turning my buttery southern brightness all northern blue and porky.

I remembered Alabama and running until my hips hurt and screaming until I was out of breath with joy. Because there I was warm and everybody knew me. There was a white sun glowing behind the pines. Crickets droning in the quiet. You could walk in the nights fearlessly, and the days were full of red clay and green fields for the eyes. Not like this place. Here you had to kick over a can, toe the trash on the curb, and try to forget the grime and sadness on the edges of everything. What green I learned to see survived between the cracks and along the worn edges of pavement. And it grew up dark, dusty, and twisted.

From the top of the school steps looking east in the winter, I felt small, like when I was in kindergarten down south and forced to sit in the back of the assembly hall to watch the school play. The bigger kids in front were always standing up. They were dominating shadows blocking the play, the light from the bright construction-paper fantasy onstage. I was too little and too afraid then to make them sit down so I could see. So now all the great buildings before me off West Madison seemed like they would never sit down or sway like those Alabama pines to let the sun through. And, then twelve years old, I would never see the sunrise over Lake Michigan until I was nearly eighteen.

So I stood there, looking for something beautiful in the silver wisps gathering in the afternoon sky above the school ground, and it reminded me of the long, clear roads in Alabama. We'd be riding in the back of Daddy's pickup, and the pine and spruce looked like they hung from the heavens like curtain fringe. The sun pounded friendly-like on our faces as we juggled around to the road's rhythm. Through the back window of the cab, I'd see Daddy's head and the dark sweat stains ringing the crown of his brown hat, the lighted Lucky Strike poking from his fingers as they gripped the steering wheel, his shimmering blue knuckles, the flying ash.

On third Fridays in the summer, it seemed like all our people in the county gathered at Uncle Ned's and Aunt Pat's for a party. About sundown, we'd come to this little, weathered, white frame house to eat smokehouse ham and biscuits at the pine picnic table covered with a red vinyl cloth. Uncle Ned always strung up his Christmas lights and everything had an amber, nightclub glow— even the fussy chickens, the dogs lounging around, and the hogs that grunted and belched contentedly in the pen back of the house. The song "Finger-poppin' Time" played over and over on the old RCA console in the house. While the cardplayers laughed, loudly slapping down diamonds and hearts, others would dance. The grown folks always looked like they were struggling when they danced, holding each other tight, the sun-bleached clothing on their backs stained with sweat. We kids would dance, too, and dash into the darkness of the adjoining fields to watch the party from a distance.

We watched the men build a great fire in one of Uncle Ned's barrels. They'd drop in great pieces of bark and coax out a flame that nipped and sweetened the velvet air of those summer nights. It was the signal to move in, of welcome, and we kids came running to the gathering around the barrel like little mosquitoes. They never passed us Uncle Ned's moonshine, but there were plenty of gold teeth and pink gums to see. And there was the warmth of big round arms with friendly fingers that fussed with the coarse braids in your hair and called you "baby." All those faces, offended if you didn't look them in the eye and smile. A child could be wide-eyed and innocent. Eyes could be clear and bright. Laughter, open and free.

I knew just where LaNell came from. I saw her when she first moved into the graystone across the street, slowly climbing the steps, staring around and looking surprised by all the winter.

"I betcha this is the first time she seen snow," I whispered to Ma Dear as we peeked secretly through our frosted window. I knew the look on her face. I remembered when Ma Dear and I first got out of Union Station and stepped into knee-deep snow. To me it meant something. When I first felt cold coming up through the sidewalk and saw all these apartments with only windows—no doors—like eyes caged and bolted, I knew it meant trouble. I knew that LaNell wondered what she was getting into —what she was doing here. So when the next day came, which was her first day at school, I asked her.

"Our Papa died," she said, "and so we came to be with our people in the north." She had that happy, talky, friendly way—the way the people are down south. She came from the kind of people who were used to looking you straight in the eye. She was small, but she was alert and wiry, this LaNell. She was dressed real neat, bright and pretty. She wore a nice white scalloped sweater. She smelled well-scrubbed and pure, like baby lotion, and her socks were very clean. She scared me a little when she looked me in the eye. I hadn't seen that for a while. Not since I had made my point the year before and I had to repeat the sixth grade for it. So I was feeling clumsy and inferior next to this girl. She reminded me of what seemed to be a better time, so I liked her. At least she came from a place where people knew some kind of peace. Where people had the decency to leave you alone.

Decency. Ma Dear liked to work that word.

"Decency," she'd hiss. "Decency. These people up here done forgot all about decency."

"Ma Dear, you been up north a long time," I'd say. "What you miss about down south?"

"The colors" was all she'd say, and fade into the dark silence of her room that smelled like camphor and rose petals. From then on I learned that sadness was keeping things to myself. I didn't dare tell Ma Dear about my own fights at school.

It was nice to have that moment there with LaNell because she was a person who didn't know the score. She talked to me off and on the rest of the day. I decided to be her secret friend. It was nice—but I stayed alert for the first sign of trouble.

It happened the next day. It was just before noon recess, and we were milling around the hallway preparing to go out to the playground. I saw this stupid girl named Tasha all up in LaNell's face. Then she grabbed LaNell's sweater, and LaNell pushed her away and started walking in my direction. The bell shrilled. Tasha and her little group of watchers stampeded out of the door for the playground. LaNell looked trapped, her face full of anger and bewilderment. She looked at me with those innocent eyes and said, "Why does that girl want to kick my behind? I don't know her. Why she want to fight?!"

I sensed LaNell was more surprised by Tasha's bizarre behavior than she was actually afraid to fight her.

"Look what she done to my sweater." She showed me a rip along the knitted shoulder seam. That meant even more trouble when she got home. But LaNell, more angered by the trouble Tasha's bullying had caused her, followed the flow of children into the playground. I saw her charge into a tight swarm of children circling Tasha. I rushed after her, pushing shoulders and elbows out of my way. Everybody was shouting and laughing. I got through in time to see LaNell nailing Tasha to the asphalt, cold smoke blowing out of her mouth, tears and snot smearing her face. One of our teachers wrestled between them and untangled their bodies. The children shrieked like birds as LaNell and Tasha were hurried off to Miss Kruger's office.

At first, I was going to wait for her after school, but when she didn't come back to class that afternoon, I knew Miss Kruger had sent her home. I needed to tell her that it wasn't over yet—that the worst was yet to come. But when I got home, LaNell's house was locked up tight. I asked Ma Dear if she had seen anyone, but she claimed she saw and heard nothing. I couldn't phone her because she didn't have one, and Ma Dear wouldn't let me go out to knock on her door. That night, I slept with my head against my knees, reliving LaNell's predicament as if it were my own. I wondered if she got a whipping for her sweater.

■ In the morning, I saw LaNell in the school playground with her face pressed against the hurricane fence. The early sun highlighted her woolly braids and plastic barrettes. Her face was scorched with the kind of life-threatening concern uncommon for a child. She was drawn and ashy, but her strength was in her anger. Her small knuckles gripped the fence wires when I told her more was to come. Tasha was just sent to test her out. Now there was this other, bigger girl, Rosalind, who wanted to fight her.

"Who are these people? What kinda place is this?" she asked. "Why can't you just go to school and mind your own business? Why these people want to try to jump on you all the time?"

"Yeah, they crazy all right. But that's the way they use to runnin' everybody around here, and just cause you new and they think you dumb and from down south, they can run you. But since you got Tasha and they know you can fight back, ain nobody gonna mess with you but Rosalind."

"That big, goonie-lookin' girl? She look like a full-grown woman."

"She act like one, too. I think something is really wrong with her mind. I see her hangin' out over there where those men be at— over by that barrel in the lot. Ma Dear beat my behind for just standing over there one time. She say, 'That ain no welcome barrel, girl. It ain like down south. Decent girls ain got no business hangin' round over there.' But this Rosalind, see, I think she killed a baby."

"Naw."

"And she known to carry a knife. She run all the stupid little people around here. Even boys scared of her."

"Why she want to stab me?"

"She don't know no other way to be."

"Well, why don't she mess with you then?"

"They did when I first got here. They came after me in a bunch. I mean they followed me down the street to my house—callin' me country and callin' my mama all out her name."

"What did you do? Did you tell Miss Kruger?"

"Who you gon tell? You heard what she said to you. Shit. That old white woman is scared of these little wild niggers, too. I made a pact with myself that nobody was ever gon call my mama out her name. So I went in the house one day they was chasin' me and I got me a butcher knife and some hot chicken grease off the stove and I went out there where they was standin' in front of my house. And I didn't care who saw me. I started flinging that hot grease. They thought I was crazy and they knew I meant business—nobody wanted to come up against that grease. Nobody mess with me ever since then."

"I don't like this place."

"They don't neither. But they don't know it."

"I don't like this fightin'."

"I didn't neither, but it something you got to do—unless you want to end up like Tasha and them—pickin' on folks for ol' Rosalind."

"That big-ass goonie."

"Yeah."

"And she carry a knife."

And with that, LaNell drifted off. She left me standing by the hurricane fence. I knew how her day would be—long, torturous, and lonely. She was a small person. The only thing big about her seemed to be her spirit. I hoped that she would run away and not be around after school.

As the school day came to a close and the time of the fight drew near, the memories and meaning of where I had come from grew stronger. I had to strike a blow for decency. I remember being mad about not being able to be a child anymore. I could not show my innocent eyes or easy smile. Maybe those kids growing up here didn't understand it, but I knew LaNell did. It took only twenty-four hours for them to worry a hole in her face. I had decided that by the time that dismissal bell rang I was not going to allow my conscience or my spirit to freeze like dull snow on a sidewalk. I decided to take on this second fight to keep these animals from getting the upper hand. If "we" didn't win, at least "we" had to raise doubts in everybody's mind about their power over us. If we didn't, the battle would never end with Rosalind.

So there I was, standing at the top of the school steps looking down at LaNell. She had wasted no time getting outside. I admired that. Underneath, I knew she wanted to cry, but instead of despair I saw a mask of anger rise and swallow her face. She was going through. She was sending whatever little girl was left in her back to Alabama, because she couldn't really live in this place. She had no idea of what she was getting into. I walked down the steps and stood at her side.

"Button your coat up. And put your gloves on," I said. "She really got a knife. Whatever you do—don't let them get your coat off or she'll stick you." I looked down. In the chill, she was wearing some little doll shoes with lace socks and rubbing her knees together.

"I know where she keep her knife. I'll go for the knife. You go for the rest."

LaNell's eyes softened for a moment as if realizing she had been given a great gift. "I want them to say, 'You see that LaNell Thomas? Don't fuck wid her. She crazy!'" And we bolted down the street, eluding the patches of ice on the pavement, running, running until our hips hurt—through debris and children yelling wildly, toward the vacant lot that was a half-block from the playground. Ahead stood Rosalind, who, at nearly six feet tall, towered over the other children. She was gathering her court near the flaming barrel.

Only two or three men were nearby, ignoring the onrush of unruly children. I remember how they moved so slowly in relation to our speed. I felt as if we were flying toward the flame they were building with old newspapers, two-by-fours, and peanut shells. The misty blue smoke rose against the growing shadows of the afternoon. Their leathered hands trembled as they picked in the ashes with sticks, coaxing the flame, paying little mind to the seriousness of what was about to go down among a bunch of little schoolgirls.

Rosalind seemed caught off guard by our confidence and boldness. I guess she didn't expect me to be in it. She still carried a scar on her hand where I had tossed the chicken grease at her. I immediately went for her coat pocket and snatched out the knife with its worn handle and shiny blade. I heard the smack of LaNell's knuckles land against the bones of Rosalind's face. Rosalind fell to the cold slush and mud. I bounced my shoe off her thigh while LaNell ate up the big girl's head and face with rapid blows.

"Git this bitch off me! Git this bitch off me!" Rosalind screamed to the others, who had held themselves back to enjoy the show. But, before they could respond and we'd be grossly out-numbered, I grabbed LaNell's arm and forced her to run with me into the street. Nobody followed. They just stood there looking in awe. The men of the barrel, who had paused to notice our assault for that quick moment, chuckled among themselves as Rosalind struggled to find her feet. The fight was over. The children scat-tered like last autumn's leaves. The lot belonged to the men of the barrel again and fell silent. Their flames popped and arched, taking a final snip at the cold blue air.

Her Crowning Glory

The day I was baptized was like any other Sunday when I'd help Ma Dear with her bathing and dressing. I was to wait at her dusty dressing table until I was called. When I heard my name at last, I had to rise and enter the moist enclosure of her barren bathroom to find her dripping hand extended, her shiny fingers seeking my shoulder. Her palm dug into my small muscles as I steadied myself. While she elevated her soapy body, rivulets trickled from its valleys and folds. The water in the tub sloshed, coughed, and gurgled. She paused to make sure her feet were secure, then, carefully, she pulled one shaky leg from the water. At one point her weight was totally on me as her dribbling foot jerked, then lowered itself to the dry white towel I had placed on the cool floor. Secured. She moved her second foot.

She fussed under her breath. Her breath was landing on my face. She said that I could never move fast enough for her—or anticipate her thoughts. She hated giving directions, and I hated concentrating on her needs just as much. I hated having to find things she had hidden in that room of hers, the one that smelled of camphor and rose petals.

I rubbed a towel across her back, and she claimed I did it too hard. She snatched the towel and pushed me aside as she staggered into her room and plopped her wide behind on the side of her bed. I stood by and watched her finish toweling her spindly legs and swollen hips. She rolled on her side to wipe her lower back. I reached forward to help her.

"Naw—don't help me, silly girl!" she said "Just get me my powder from over there!"

She leaned back on the bed and, lifting both legs, she toweled under her butt. Then, rolling up, she tugged at the flabby mound cresting her belly, dabbing and buffing the crevices under the great pouch. Her midriff looked like a brown buttoned pillow mounted by long sloping breasts, mutton-chop arms adorned with a half-moon scar where she had once been burned, and assorted pits and dimples. I had turned to the dressing table and couldn't distinguish the powder container from the morass of fancy clutter in the half-light. She had all the brown window shades drawn, blocking out the morning brightness.

"Don't you see it?" she insisted. "It's there!"

I didn't see it. But I reached for it, pretending to know where it was. Just to silence her. My eyes, my heart raced. Just to silence her.

"Not there, stupid. There! There!"

I looked back at her, my hands reaching and fumbling over things on the dressing table.

"What are you looking at me for?!" Her eyes widened. "Oh I'm sick of you!" She slung the towel around and cracked me on the arm. "Get out of the way. Get me those things over there—on the chair!"

I went over to the chair and gathered her underthings. I held them as she searched the dressing table for the container of powder. Not finding it there, she sat back in disgust on the bed and studied me for a moment. Then she shifted her left foot and tipped a container of pale pink dusting powder over on the floor. As she bent to pick it up, I wanted to kick her square in the butt. Once she had retrieved it, she did not look at me, but began systematically sprinkling her limbs, her underarms, and balding pubic area. She kept her eyes away from mine as she examined the clothing in my arms and snatched off the broad cotton panties. She rolled on her back and thrust her legs through them, carefully fitting the band around her swollen waist. Then she unraveled the bra, standing and bending forward like a Japanese sumo; she poured her ample brown breasts like coffee into the great white cups.

"Go get my uniform," she said, plopping once more on the bed to roll her beige stockings on. Carefully I placed her silk slip beside her and walked around the bed to the gaping darkness of the closet. The air in the closet smelled like tobacco, overripe grapes, and allspice. Her white church uniform was secured under a protective plastic garment bag pinned to the wire and cardboard hanger by tiny gold safety pins. She wore it every Sunday she sat on the Mothers' Board and for first Sunday baptisms. I reached under the plastic and removed each pin, closed one, and put it in my mouth. I pinched the metal with my teeth. I remembered Ma Dear and I did this whenever we peeled onions to prevent tears.

Feeling the cool clicking of the pin between my clenching teeth, I swooped the uniform into my arms like it was Cinderella or Sleeping Beauty. I swirled around and around, enjoying the freshness I stirred in the purple air of the room, a room so groggy and full of sleep, sweat, and the light rose perfume of her dusting powder. As I whirled around in that very small space, feeling the warm, delicate cling of the plastic garment bag, I struck my toe against the base of the bed. I anticipated the pain.

"What in the world are you doing?" said Ma Dear. "My dress is not a plaything. You crazy as Deenie MacDaniel! Come here and help me fasten my bra. Why aren't you dressed?"

But I was dressed. She just couldn't see under the housecoat I was wearing. Ma Dear always had me put my dress on last so that I wouldn't mess it up. I had everything on but my dress. The housecoat was pink with a round lacy collar and covered with white hearts. My hair was pressed, pulled, and rubber-banded into a little black pigtail cinched on the end by a white barrette. Wavy bobby pins kept the sides of my hair from jutting out like blades of black grass. My breasts were not impressive yet, so I wore a white undershirt, white slip, and tights, and my black patent leather dress shoes with the Minnie Mouse bows.

I draped the dress carefully on the bed and forgot about dancing with fairy-tale beauties. Ma Dear hunched over while I fastened the little metal claws on the back of her bra. The safety pin clicked against my teeth.

"Get that thing out of your mouth. You don't need that pin in your mouth."

I slipped it into my pocket.

"Come round here," she ordered. She leaned forward and began sniffing me to make sure I wasn't musty. Then she sat back and studied me some more.

"Thought I caught a whiff of somethin'."

My cheeks tingled and my head raced. Then she spun me around when I finally met her approval.

"I just want to make sure. I'm not havin' you embarrassin' me. Now go put your dress on."

As I ran to my room, I thought about the notorious Deenie MacDaniel, who was our neighbor and a sister in our church. Ma Dear detested crazy people. She was never fond of surprises, and

Deenie MacDaniel was always full of them. First testing Ma Dear's Christian patience when they sang in the Pastor's Choir, Deenie MacDaniel was a bundle of contradictions. Ma Dear was forced to stand next to her in the soprano section. To Ma Dear, Deenie MacDaniel bumped against her needlessly. Or sometimes she'd recoil violently from the most innocent touch, accusing Ma Dear of trying to be sexual with her. It got worse during one choir rehearsal following an argument mediated by the choir director: quickly spinning out of control, Deenie MacDaniel marched to the end of the center, consecrated aisle, bent over, lifted her skirt, and patted her naked behind at Ma Dear and the other members in the choir stand. Ma Dear threatened to change churches. Pastor Ware counseled patience.

Deenie MacDaniel could have been a tall, bronze showgirl, but she was the mother of nine children and the wife of a dreamer, musician, and handyman. She was under heavy strain. The strain meant people putting her in hospitals, having nappy-headed children with no shoes, episodes of walking outside naked, sometimes balancing one of her small babies on top of her head like an African urn. Those were moments I thought she looked so bizarre, but so beautiful. She would be smiling as if she were in touch with some great vital force that had pulled her out of her clothes and made her walk before the world so we could see her great brown primeval beauty. She walked. Everybody gawked, and Ma Dear called the police. Ma Dear's eyes would be transfixed on her, but unlike the other members of the church, not one modicum of pity could be found in them. Ma Dear's eyes would freeze over, watering and blinking only when she turned away.

Once my white dress was on, I returned to Ma Dear's room to find her fully clothed and primping in the mirror. She had yet to raise the shades in her room, so she was grooming herself by the dim glow of a little angel lamp on her dresser.

"Now," she said, noting my return. "Get me my new hat."

With excitement I reached for a large hatbox she had positioned on top of the chest of drawers. I placed it on the bed and opened the great oval top.

"Have you washed your hands?" she snapped.

"Yes ma'am," I lied, scooping the large lovely bonnet into my tainted hands. It was a cornucopia of weaved whiteness, a flying swan, ornamental blossoms, and grape leaves whirled into a crown with a brim like a ship's bow. I tugged the ball of paper tissue that held the crown's shape and let it drop into the box with the price tag. I assumed my station behind Ma Dear as she gazed upon her own face, which looked suspended in the mirror. Like a royal lady in waiting, I held the great white hat. Raising the hat in my hands, I noticed I was only a dim silhouette in her reflecting glass, her little angel lamp not illuminating me at all. Her newly powdered face and great white shoulders filled the dark mirror like an evening moon. She raised her hands, and I placed her crowning glory on her fingertips, then she lowered it to her head with the slow precision of a coronation. I watched all this while trying to discern the whites of my eyes in her mirror, with little success. Once Ma Dear's portrait was sufficient in her own eyes, she adjusted her hat with a tap of her finger and sighed.

■ Cousin Claude was coming to pick us up. I waited in the living room with a three-day-old sheet cake and Ma Dear's large-print Bible. I had wanted a taste of that cake so badly when it was first made. But Ma Dear never allowed it. I was told not to touch that cake until the proper time. So there it sat, under transparent wrap on the milk-white surface of the kitchen table, smelling of lemon and cane sugar, gathering dust on the surface of the cellophane. I was always wiping around it with the dishrag, pressing and tucking in the loose ends. Now here it sat, next to me with an added blanket of aluminum foil, with no fragrance at all and hardened icing. The smells of bacon and bath soap were still heavy in the air, and the windows frosted lightly from the humidity. Ma Dear told me not to jump around because I tended to give off an odor if I got sweaty. I sat and meditated on Jesus and all the things that were planned for this most important day in my life.

Ma Dear entered the room, studied me for a moment, then disappeared into her bedroom. She reappeared holding a white ribbon between her fingers. It was one that had decorated the hatbox. She smoothed my unruly strands of hair. Then I felt her fingers working and designing a bow for my lone pigtail. She had roses in her skin and peppermint rolling around in her mouth. When money was short, she used vanilla extract and citrus peelings. But on this day, instead of a smooth store-bought mint, she offered me the natural bitters of an orange skin to sanctify my mouth. She turned me around and brushed the corners of my lips.

"Smile," she said. I showed her my teeth. She smiled back, then pressed her warm, dry lips into my left cheek.

"Ma Dear, you look so pretty," I said. She had added a corsage of silk flowers, rouge, and a set of pearl earrings.

"So do you," she answered. "God bless you this morning, child."

■ "Wow," said Claude, soaking in Ma Dear's noble appearance. "Whose baptism is it today? You look like you going to see the king."

"Don't walk your Auntie up to heaven so soon," she warned. From the front seat, she reached into her purse and handed me a starburst of peppermint. I was in the backseat of Claude's Chevrolet with the sheet cake. I was happy because something special was going to happen to me. It would be a long Sunday: first Sunday school, then morning service, then dinner, then baptism in the long afternoon. All that mattered to Ma Dear was that I meet the setting sun as a full-fledged Christian and member of the Greater Nicodemus' Rest Missionary Baptist Church. But it was more important to me that something was actually happening to me and that there was a real possibility that some great secret of my heart would rear her head—and make herself known.

Would the world have new colors when I came out of the water? Would I, like some, be seized by the spirit while I was submerged and be driven up from the depths like a holy missile? I smiled to myself, thinking once again about Deenie MacDaniel. About how Pastor Ware in his big fishing boots had dipped her down in the water and how she claimed to have become filled with the holy spirit and bucked and breached like a whale. She almost emptied the baptismal pool, drenching the choir pews beneath it. I laughed to myself. Deenie MacDaniel tickled me.

■ Outside the car window, I could see we were approaching the little On This Rock Holiness Church. I had asked Ma Dear if I could go to that church with my friend LaNell. LaNell was in that church all day long on Sunday and into the evening. If I was going by, I would see her enter the storefront temple where it was warm and bright inside with driving rhythms. She was swallowed into a school of clapping hands and tambourines. Memphis blues chords dangled like rainbows.

"I don't want to see you hanging out there," said Ma Dear. "You can't serve two masters."

Looking in I could see the place heating up for a praise dance. I imagined LaNell's feet thumping the floor with all the others, doing steps. I wanted to join the sanctified church. I wanted to dance. When the Holy Ghost touched me, I wanted to do more than the Missionary Baptist could. They could fall out, stretch out, clear out, and run out—but not dance. There was no dancing at the Greater Nicodemus' Rest Missionary Baptist Church. That was for "those holy sanctified folk" just to keep up noise, Ma Dear told me. But there was a part of me that was happy in the presence of the drum, in the presence of holy dancers whose bodies stiffened in elegant contortions, searching out steps, unique steps, steps all their own. With rapid sticks and cymbals bashing the air, I had watched some throw their heads back while others dipped fluidly, arching their bodies, pumping their legs forward to the beat.

"Oh Lord, have mercy!" Ma Dear's sigh was seasoned with anger. Claude was pulling up to Greater Nicodemus' Rest. He seemed to catch what Ma Dear was looking at. His eyes jutted to the backseat and captured mine. Ma Dear was grinding her teeth.

"Sometimes I wish that I could just go crazy! Go stark-raving crazy!"

A chattering flock of church members was hanging outside and gradually entering the red brick structure. There was the usual traffic congestion, honking horns and huddles of the freshly groomed greeting one another. We saw Deenie MacDaniel surrounded by her brood of restless children, squatting on the church steps, adjusting the dress of one of her smallest, who was wedged between her knees. She was smiling, oblivious to the condescending stares of the church members stepping around her. She wore a full gypsy skirt, a graying white blouse, and a hat that looked exactly like Ma Dear's.

That was the beginning of our long day. Deenie MacDaniel's hat seemed to knock the wind out of Ma Dear, and, as I helped her from the car, she gripped my arm so tight I almost screamed with pain. Deenie MacDaniel's kids were loud, and eager to point out the similarities. Deenie MacDaniel beamed with flattery. Ma Dear was boiling with rage, but she maintained her Christian aplomb and walked through the crowd the best way she could. She had invested too much in that hat to take it off. Then her second indignity arrived during the meal that followed the morning service. The sisters in the basement kitchen found that the great sheet cake she had so carefully prepared three days before was riddled with green mold.

Well, I thought, as Ma Dear's fingers prepared me for baptism, I guess I'm the only pair of eyes around here that she thinks are not laughing at her. She sought them, she needed them without an ounce of mockery. And so I gave them to her. I brushed my fingers, pressed their cool tips to the tender socket around each white eyeball, pressed and pulled. It was my ultimate act of love.

■ I had to be helped into the baptismal pool, though. Until my spiritual eyes grew I had to rely on what other people told me. They told me I was wearing white socks, a white gown, and a white swimming cap. They told me the spirit was so high that Deenie MacDaniel broke into a dance and almost tore off all her clothes. They had to tell me because I couldn't remember the cold climb of chlorine water against my skin, the rubber smell of Pastor Ware's boots, my going down and being raised up through the water. Ma Dear had to tell me because I couldn't remember. There are only these little marks on my forehead—little scratches that remain from the clawed feet of some descending dove.

Fetish

A shoe is valued highly if it is:

Placed in a man's hand.

Thrown into silhouette by a lamp.

Seen as an imprint in fresh snow.

. . .

I dig my heels in when I walk.
I grind my pumps down to the nails,
can't wait to wear them out,
just to get Woody to glue on taps.
When I pick up those red spikes with vinyl bows,
I'm going to put a whole lot of Estée Lauder
on my feet.
              See, at Woody's Shoe Repair,
he gives your kid (whining mamma mamma,
shrieking like a jungle bird
while swinging on your purse) a dime
for jawbreakers; he shows you the heel,
shows how he worked it at the lathe.
Then he kneels and slips your sweaty shoe
right on your foot—says, "Only one way
to try it out," and waltzes you around
the shop. Holds your waist and gallops
you in circles until dust flies
up from Red Wings, Buster Browns no one ever

picked up. You want to ask
about newspaper clippings on the wall:
Woody in boxing trunks, his arm
around Ali, Leon Spinks;
Woody winning a boodle in the CA lottery
Big Spin. You want to ask
about the pink scar on his temple.
You really want to drag him off
into a back room full of shoe leather
and wear that man out. But you don't.
You paint your toenails Scarlet
Flamingo. And wear out your shoes. Save them
claim tickets for what's yours.

.   .   .

On her night off, Grandmother Kathryn dragged
the lawn chairs out. She propped up her feet.
It took pruning shears and all my weight
to cut through the yellow nail that stood
up like a wooden spoon from her big toe.
Thirty years back, while cutting out soles
at International Shoe Company in West Plains,
she'd dropped a shank on her foot.
She settled down after that.

.   .   .

We hit Carlsby, Nevada, after midnight,
nearly out of gas and the gas cap frozen up.
The woman at the pumps was locking up.
She said this wasn't any place for a gal
and her son to sleep in a truck.
She'd call her boyfriend to monkey-wrench
the cap off.
                 Only one casino was lit
down the hill. For what I know, Carlsby's
a lovely place in early light,
vining clematis and hollyhocks shooting up

in great brakes around snug bungalows.
At midnight, though, it's wind and red dust
shuddering the truck, a train horn bleating,
and a tired man pulling tools out of his Nova,
plying the stubborn cap with a wrench.
He wore boxers and work shoes
full of so many small holes
that I saw his pale feet.

"Why do people live here?" I asked.
"Silver mining," she said.
"The big companies do pretty good."

She wore low-heeled pumps.

. . .

The first time we went to bed,
I wore a red-dragon kimono. His
was blue. Before we'd done it once,
he showed me all the positions
he'd like to try
in the book of Chinese erotic art:

Upside-down Clouds,

The Jade Stalk Knocks at the Door,

Penetrating the Cords of the Lute,

The Leaping White Tiger.

The ladies' feet curved like tiny pony hooves.
He said that connoisseurs
of bound feet could name fifty-eight
varieties: "Lotus Petal,"
"New Moon," "Gracious Salutation."

"The Golden Lotus" was reserved

for the smallest foot, three inches
at the most. We looked at pages
of Golden Lotuses in embroidered
silk baby boots. Then he showed me
how to raise my foot and bend
over until my hair swept the floor.

"What's this one called,
The Guppy Drowns in the Moat?"

"That's it.
Bend over."

    . . .

My friend, who had worked
at an orphanage in Honduras,
said to me:

I saw a child's shoe in the street.
When I picked it up, I saw the foot
was still in it.

    . . .

After the police beat back
crowds from Rudolph Valentino's
wake, they found 28 shoes, umbrellas,
and torn sleeves in the streets.

    . . .

A shoe is valued highly if it is:

Placed on a man's lap.

Photographed in an alley.

Seen as an imprint in flesh.

El Día de los Muertos

HORNITOS, CALIFORNIA
for Kevin

Sometimes I took the drive alone, past
the burned flour and woolen mills
near Lake McSwain. In the summer
the ranch women of Agua Fría, Indian Gulch,
watch the sky for fire planes banking
out of Fresno, away from the high Sierras.
Days after the grass fires have gone out,
the blackened foothills smolder
near the road's edge.
                    I was amazed by the burn line,
so close to ranch houses, where women still
hung wet bedding on the clotheslines.
                            Sometimes,
hugging my car around abrupt bends,
the window down, the sweet, burnt wind
whipping my hair, I wanted to be a ranch woman,
leaning her face against the veranda screen,
the bright unstoppable fire, a fermata,
holding her life, kindling
the one memory that flares briefly for her then:

a late-night kitchen, a yellow table she sits at
with spiced tea, the dark rain beating
at the windowpane. Is that all she can wish for,
rain? She watches the red fire curl over the berm
of the trenches, her husband's last attempt
to stop the flames. Her baby wakes
now in its bassinet.
                   And this can't happen.
The ranch woman packs up the pickup.
She gets out.

Kevin, this time I wanted to take you with me,
to see the winding procession of candles,
the lit faces climbing the hill, Francisco's
grave, as if it could have meaning for you.
In this photograph, you stand by an hornito on the hill;
hornitos, for "little ovens," the dark adobe graves.
You hold the candle so close to your face.

The fine incisions high on your buttocks
still bleed and hurt. I can't touch you,
slip my hand into the hollow of your back,
the way I want to. It will be two days
before your surgeon calls to say the word
we each think quietly to ourselves that day:
Leukemia. Like a chant, like Alleluia.

We gathered our candles when the light fell,
climbed with the others. A cedar fence post marked
Francisco's grave. I put my candle on it.
I wanted to tell you about him then,
but the Spanish mass, prayers for Doña Calendaria,
drifted toward the goat fields. I watched
each face take on its own quiet light.

When I was five years old, my parents
brought me to Hornitos nearly every Sunday.
Francisco Salazar ran the jail museum,
a one-celled granite block. It held
a few joss sticks, a "Burning Judas" doll,
a lynching rope. I remember touching Francisco's
white trimmed beard, wearing his prospector's hat.

He told me about Rosie Martinez's Fandango Hall,
all underground, with wagon-wheel lanterns, an entrance
to Joaquin Murietta's secret cave.
Francisco saw Murietta's head,
pickled in whiskey in a jar in San Francisco,
right before the 1906 fire. The face
was bloated and the long hair swirled

against the glass.
                      I always begged Francisco
for the story of la Patricia,
a dance hall girl known as Shoo-Fly,
a song she sang at the fandango hall.
She had a daughter, who at just my age
died in a fever. The daughter lay in an hornito
on the hill. Shoo-Fly saved fandango tips
for a better grave, one dynamited into the rockbed.
She opened the hornito herself, prying out bricks.
Her daughter's small bones crumbled in her hands.
The next day, in the town plaza, Shoo-Fly set
herself on fire and danced herself to death.

I wanted to tell you these things, Kevin.
But it was quiet, and we stood with los muertos.
I didn't know then how the disease
would require its own litany of rage;
how your quiet sentence, "Loretta,

I don't want to die," would become the one cruel
motto of our lives. How in the night
you would take out that rage, first on objects.
How I would sweep glass, plaster sheetrock, calm
alarmed neighbors, and then, finally, lock my son
and myself in his room.
                      Did I think a woman
couldn't leave a dying man?
                      I have one box
of your things. I'm shipping them, with these photographs.
It's cooler here in the Midwest.
I am driving slowly behind the Amish buggies.
I'm taking my son to the river.
In November homeowners rake leaves on their driveways.
They prod small fires they watch over.
The fires flare up and flare down.

Soup

My mother bones hot chicken with her hands,
I pat the board with flour, roll egg noodle dough
out thin. We both unbutton collars, use kitchen mitts
to wave off steam, the reek of onions, heat.
When she fans the pot lid back and forth,
drops in the meat, I breathe carrots, celery,
whole tomatoes brewing in their skins.
Now we can "let it set" until a fork can pierce
a carrot through. We untie aprons, rinse fingers
underneath the spout, take tall ice teas
to the window room: sycamores, lilacs, plum.
Still safe from street sweepers, vagrant dogs,
the man with no shoes who, this morning, flashed
a peace sign at us and continued down the road,
my son ploughs around the lavender rose.
Tiffany, cousin Sue's girl, spades Johnson grass,
chews chickweeds.   *You keep an eye on her,*
Mother says. We both know what she means.
Uncle Zesker, sixty-two, boozed and weaving in the lanes,
had snapshots in his wallet. *Tiffanies little*
pussie, Tiffany eating head, the ink inscriptions
said. "Six years for violating a special trust"
with his granddaughter. Now the family
talks the photos up: her small body spread
against chenille bed.   At the trial, the girls spoke up.
Aunt Sherry, Gayla, Catherine-Ann, girls
with children of their own. Each woman stated for the record
a hand across a breast, a fondled crotch,
the words, "It's like a baby's bottle.
Suck." *Sometimes she throws herself*
against the rug and screams. Mother sips her tea.
I watch Tiffany's shadowed lap where my son piles

an ocean of plum leaves.

                         Did he touch you?
Mother shoots at me, her glasses strange
and misty from the steam.

                         Swimming lessons at the lake,
green one-piece, waves that still rolled
their sickness over my bed when I lay down to sleep.
Zesker's grip between my thighs tight and warm underwater.
Sunsuits with elastic legs.

                         I shake my head, *Not ever,*
and rise to dump the noodles in the broth.
When the light seeps off to other neighborhoods,
and Mrs. Kirby, blue hair and thin housecoat,
raises her sprinkler key to chase the kids inside,
I'll open the door, brush sawdust from their pants,
scrub faces, my son's veined and transparent as onion skin,
Tiffany's flushed with play.
And why did I come all this distance, and too late,
that man already put away? To stir soup with mother?
To watch a small girl's lap fill with leaves?
Mother is climbing on a chair for the special
Blue Willow. We'll dip up large noodles
curled in hot broth, chicken, onions.
A gift for the children: something good
in nice bowls.

Hayward, California, 1968

Grandmother lifts pots from each blue moon
of flame, peppers spinach, adds mustard
and brown sugar to the beans. She slips
on oven mitts, waves off the heat to baste
the roast. Soon she will untie apron,
listen for her boyfriend's dumptruck to grind
gravel in the lot.
                She will open the back screen
and call my name, over and over, in sad syllables
that mean as much to me as the faint organ bells
of St. Joseph's, or the syllables of blackbirds
swooping off through flecked sky.
                     I will see
her there, in the kitchen cluttered
with Kewpie dolls, blown-glass dogs, Aunt Jemima spoons,
the light dim from the resin-grapes lamp,
the kitchen and grandmother flooded in sepia,
like a curled photograph. I will see
the glittery paint-by-numbers Last Supper,
the lilac wallpaper brown with roach eggs
and dog piss.
            If I climb the twenty-four
stairs above Groveland Market, its owner, Miss Chin,
busy in her own kitchen with ribs and stir-fry,
I will see my grandmother cradling lemons,
slapping off flies.
                But nothing can persuade
me to go in; not Pellengrini's auction yard,
all locked up; not the turbines that churn up
clouds of late summer; not the sky burning
its last strands of violet, purple,
livid pink.
            I am eight. My granny skirt drags
in the dirt. My bobbed hair is wild straw.

I scout Pellengrini's chain-link for busted
TV tubes, knobs of Quasars, rusted spikes.
I saw at tendrils of morning glories, fill
my pockets with red leaves and rocks.

A month ago my father dropped me off.
Before he backed the Buick down the drive,
he cranked the window, said, *Be good, Katydid.*
I'll get you when I can.
I haven't heard from him.

Soon Pickett's truck will lurch and grumble
in the yard. One by one, like Main Street lamps,
the stars come on. Next to the auction yard
a Texaco lights up. Headlights glow
on Groveland.
                    The first night, grandmother
fed me a mug of chicken broth and stars.
She showed me her hand-carved whatnot, mirrors
and curled mahogany. The center shelf held
a Shinto Hatey she called Buddha, squatting over
his big brown belly, his lips gold-leafed, his hands
raised above his head. She'd glued a red rhinestone
on his navel. *I rub it for good luck.*

Pickett grunted with black-and-white wrestlers on TV
and said to me, *Hey, girl, I hear your mother's*
crazy, huh? What she do to get locked up?
Later, when they fought, he called her Kathryn
and held her wrist. He swung the window wide
and tossed out the Star of David clock
and 7-Up, the cat with seven toes on each paw.
He slapped her hard.

Now, it is impossible to remember the way
a girl watched Miss Chin stock her shelves
with seaweed and black moss; impossible
to remember any thoughts at all of the mother,

the fields of tulips I passed
on the long way home with my father.

I remember the sound of the slap,
of "Kathryn," the way the letters of my own
name flew off like mourning doves. I remember
the smell of burning creosote, the cold moon floating
out, a buoy in gray clouds.
                              I remember
how I took words from Pellengrini's: *thresher,*
push mower, pump, and made up songs
I hummed to myself as I filled my heavy pockets
with pignuts.
                  I remember how my grandmother
put my hand on the Brown Buddha; how she
scrubbed and scrubbed my skirt hem.

Photo, Fable, Field Trip

Nothing is ever the same
as they said it was.
DIANE ARBUS   An Aperture Monograph

If this was not the Pierre or the Ritz,
then what does it matter, flopped in this hotel
forever, Broadway & 100th Street, *Transvestite*
at her Birthday Party, N.Y.C., 1969.

And if Arbus had to brave the back steps
to this place, the elevator broken by those
too dead on their feet to find the right floor,
it wasn't so much for the man peignoired on the bed,
or the stale indivisible cake,
or even a girl strangled without passion
with a looped lamp cord in the room below;

the photograph was, I think, a momentary home,
in the exactitude of shadows, for a woman,
an aperture and a brief scherzo of light.

And if a woman shuts off a light in one
winter-grayed valley of California, and, thinking
of the man in the photograph, then turns
to the cold window's composition of night,
it isn't for the lilac or elm to announce,
she once found her husband in fishnet stockings
alone in a room with a magazine;
                                    let the bed
keep its silence of pillows. All the woman wants
is to watch a small moon-kindled fire frost
the lawn, silver fig limbs, shadow the fence,
but a quilt is thrown back, and her man,
showered and spiced, is extending one hand.

And if this man now cups in his hands warmth
of another fire he has built in a barbecue
of a river-crossed park, his wife and son braving
the bank's burdock and thistles for keepsake
granite, then he can only wonder if the water
might take them from some perilous slope.

Down the river, past the trestle, cedars crowd
the water, trunks close together, but here,
it is nice for a woman to rest on a stump
near a rill clotting, green-spumed and water-lilied,
in the limbs of an uprooted birch, minnows rising
for skippers, darting from their water drawn circles,
pyrite pulsing with light.

                    My son bellows, *Yield
dragon, or die* to a gray log augured to the bank
and fringed with dry moss; I hold his apple,
and we believe in a Loch Ness–stalked moat.
If a stern lady rose now from the green water
and asked *Why stay?* I couldn't nod to the boy
prodding the dragon with his dagger of bark, nor
to the man, a ways off, sifting handfuls of smoke.

Soon, red-tailed hawks will rise up from their trees,
and we'll follow them into the dusk. Home,
the boy will wake only long enough to ask
who fixed the moon, and we'll carry him
to his room.
                    Alone, the man and I will rock
in the brief home of our making, then I'll sleep,
head on his breast, and wake to Sunday papers
and coffee; we'll drink from chipped yellow mugs
and read "Broom Hilda," "Wizard of Id," while outside,
a winter wind explains itself only in a tremolo
of branches, a slight swell of a flowered apron.

Justine Has a Few Words for the Marquis de Sade

For one year
after the lightning
I dreamed about women
sleeping between bread knives.

The point is

The point is

beyond the rocks. I have stopped dreaming
& whatever you want,

just want.

I have waded out today

past the silt edge

where it gets deeper.

Have peeled my suit
down past my hips.

The sunbathers baked on the rocks
can see nothing through this dark water.

You can see nothing,
not the faint scars

      under one breast.

I had a simple life,

like an old ballad:

I walked out crying
past city skylines.

I sat in a hayloft
like a maid.

I knew how to balance my pails.

I wandered the cliffs
looking for oyster scows,
Russian whalers.

I remember drunks, azaleas,
my grandmother's torn petticoats,

like drummers after a battle,
like the red satin shoe
I found in the vale.

My shoulders are cold
under water.
The sun is warm on my face.

I live in California.

Even if you follow me here

Even if you follow me here

    I remember mother
    dressing at the sink.
    Chet Atkins on the radio.

On any street
you might bump against

me   a woman straightening
her skirt   suddenly
a face you remember.

I'm the arm
moving carefully
through the roses,

the garter hitched
up
behind
the café counter.

Not
the woman parked at a Texaco
in Death Valley,

dialing your number.

Not
the woman splayed
in the vineyard.

(Never
the Troubadour's Lady
devoured by hounds.)

I like to read and sleep
after a swim.

That's my face
reading in yellow light
by the window on the third floor
above the depot.

The sky smells like geraniums.
The air grows thinner.

Your train is pulling out.

I don't own anything
but a few ribbons

& my own scars.

You can't touch them.

Your train is pulling out,
& you're on it, I said.

I wrote the book
in my lap.

I won't look up.

Reba Talks of the August Strike

When the mines work Bobby leaves a slight dip in the bed.
Now he's gone three nights to Kentucky, two to Ohio
From where the news shows coaldocks flaming up.
I search the screen for sight of his truck.
Home to sleep, it's as if he's all weight,
His body unreeled from picketing and escaping.
I have the children, the hours calling other women,
My hands chalky on the phone.
The children tumble in the high grass, try to climb the hill.
Birch, alder, elm grow furiously there for nothing.

We used to spin for hours on the couch that was his mother's
Talking of an earth righted, available.
His first picket meeting I didn't want him going.
He stopped home just to set out again with a carload to Marmet.
I flapped about, took scraps of radio as gospel,
Phoned my sister in Clendenin.
She thought little of labor strife, five years married
To a linoleum salesman, except she said they'd suffer
If the strike stretched out a month. I had one baby then,
A good girl who gravitated to the half-toothed men
As wives like me waited at the Welfare, clutching
The paper wads that spoke our payments and debts.
With those of us lucky to own a boat or a second car,
We conspired how to conceal it, worth little enough,
So food stamps were denied no one.

They got to know me as *Bobby's wife Reba*, a *radical*
In one breath. I spoke at meetings.

Sometimes a phone rings late:
'Your husband is going to be shot.'
It's women burn me up. 'Hun, you know Bobby's jamming
The blond coalminer with the big tits,'
Or 'You're taking food from my babies.'
I've learned to hold my tongue.

Each county has a few who don't know fear, the ones
The law can't touch because they've ceased respecting it.
Those raw and stupid enough, I think at times, to stand up.
When he's home we talk strategy, what the judge can do,
Or if he's in contempt again.

I tell the stories my granddad told, strikers tucked
In the hills thick as oaks, expecting machine-gunners
On the armored train, talk I stirred root beer to
In Mom's Cedar Grove Café. Truckers heading east
Or north took his stories, maps out of forgetting.
Granddad remembered, the way soda erupts with ice cream,
Mixing Mother Jones and Bill Blizzard,
Zeroing in on hunger and gunmetal.

When I first loaded the .22 the cylinder was upside down.
I inched through town to Pearl's house, the rifle hidden.
When the town cop stopped my car, he spied it.
'It's not loaded,' I lied. I didn't know. He let me go.
Later, Bobby taught me how to load, to aim, to accept the kick.
There's some backward fools about, he said. Didn't we know,
Our poodle poisoned, the porch light zinged out,
My mother cussing me on the phone I should leave this madness,
Bobby annoyed at me for showing fear.
It'll pass, I said. It did.

I've slept soundly with the double barrel
By my bed since this strike began.
I miss him in the bed.
I like to have him home nights he's not working,
Hear his breathing, feel his tossing,
Leaving himself as he sleeps, letting the earth be.

The children wake so early, unaware what striking means.
They seem to want me more. They want to climb the hill
Every chance and look for snakes, smell the tomato leaves,
Listen for the fat red birds that land this way now,
Watch the easy smoke corkscrew from the bottom houses,
To listen, listen for the silence that replaces work trains.
They want to touch my face, hold my hand, sing
The songs my grandfather taught me,
Work this waiting like the earth,
Slow for nothing, in wild tunes.

Electricity

I pass them in the halls, squatting
Or leaning to the moss-green walls,
Still drinking beer from their paper sacks.
This is night college, the union electricians.
I want to hate them uniformly room after room
Below the flags and chalkboards of yellow dust.
I want to be wanted by all of them along the lockers.
Sometimes they refuse me my name—only *teacher.*
They dig in the desks for the high school kids' leavings,
Carved longings, silver foil and clumps of hair.
The blond man sits glazed in the third row,
The pot still wiring from him.
I correct his papers easily.
He'd be good but he sees no purpose in it,
The Irish muck in him thick and bleak.
It's always men who drink or see too much who want me.
Once for a week through an apartment window I measured
A man lit by a gooseneck lamp who never spied me
As he watched the night or straightened his books.
What is this bare cold light?
At his workshop in West Orange, Edison hovered
Over his men—*muckers,* he called them—as they unwrapped
The properties of rubber, palm leaves, hemp.
They swallowed the phonograph's wail of lyric or cello
While he napped on his laboratory cot.
After work, in the soulless hours,
They chose the humid bar or the dim trek home,
Trying to assess what was luck,
What sheer power in the bonds they'd uncovered.

We Are All Girls

When my sister tells me she's seeing an old friend
Who's squandered two decades in a bottle,
I think of others I've run into lately,
How I've sorted the past too neatly
And wonder if we old friends will ever speak
Of the nights we spent behind locked doors
Touching each other's nipples, reaching
Fingers down to the girlish dark.
What scenes of intimacy, or rather fantasy,
Each wanting so much the other to be a man.
No specific man was attached to the desire,
Not then, even though we hungered
For particular boys, sometimes for the same boy.
What we sought was man, to make us
Come alive into the woman bodies we were founding
Like great nation states or massive cities
We knew even then we weren't destined to rule.

Once I wore diaphanous cloth, hankering
To join some busy harem, to be taken and lost.
If I acted this with a girlfriend, I don't recall.
Perhaps I was alone, or six, dancing borrowed steps
Around our live oaks, thirty miles from Hollywood.
I recall my mother dressing to go out—
Her silky small knees, her neck enriched by perfume,
But not smooching or fondling my father,
Perhaps because he walled off his longings.
Still she could talk sex OK.
It wasn't forbidden. But I had a fledgling
Sex life protected and sweet, illicit
Like our shoplifting trips. Not all of us stole,
Not all of us touched each other.
But now stealing rubs at a clitoris or areola,
Mixes with robbing dresses or books

Into the same teen lust. I confess, I confess.
With my girlfriends, I don't recall penetration,
I don't remember kissing, after maybe playing
Guitars or trading earrings, just the body's
Peaks—breast, the vulva's lips and mount,
And all the others asleep in the house.

Naming the Body

For a little while no one notices you. Their eyes are on Chickie,
Who hit the ball up the hill where men wave in approval.

There's Ad Waters, the Negro whose nephew got shot in Alabama,
"Executed," Ad had yelled, flapping the military condolences,

"The Army clipped him. This here's all lies." And the other men
Against the cars, cheering Chickie. The little squirt, Benny's kid
    brother,

Runs after the ball and Tito and Victor go wild, but Chickie wears
That 'it's a common occurrence' face, like he's a killer. Women puff

At the curb, carting bags of bread. "Hi Benita," they say, "how's
    your ma?"
You nod, "She's better. Aunt Penny says she'll be fit for work by
    Tuesday."

You'll be glad. She won't lie on the couch, gray like a battleship
When you get home from school, telling you no phone calls.

She must nap—because anyone's pleasure destroys her.
It's war at home, you three women. When you tell Mrs. Aintrezi

You have been to the store you expect to be called a good girl,
But what do the women in the neighborhood know of you?

You watch Chickie again. Gerald fires out of 587 for the phone.
You could shoot that girl on the other end. Or he's planning

Some break-in job, or a warehouse. It's been months since you
    talked.
Gerald was one of the first who took you to the basement at 570.

You were just a fifth-grade kid. You'd gone for a smoke, and to
    show
Each other your bodies, sex education, you called it. You felt

In the swing, having read where most Americans polled agreed
Kids need sex education, and doctors should be open with their
    patients

About diseases. Which your parents never communicate, but it was
In the paper. It was your idea. The boys from St. Joan's

Promised it'd be nice when you got bigger, down in the basement,
But they only knew this from their brothers, in high school then,

And those brothers are gone into the service now, and the boys
From St. Joan's in high school, and they'll be next. You'd be a
    looker,

These brothers prophesied like Elijah, while your mom railed
Against easy girls in Catholic schools, promiscuous, you liked

The sound of the word, Latinate, you could imagine a nun
    lisping it.
Now you are an eyelid, the men razz you on Broadway.

You went down there with Chickie and his cousin from Albemarle
    Road
Who plays the harmonica, your butt against the linoleum table

In the storage room, watched them hold their Luckies like gangsters
Or stockbrokers. His cousin cut out, so Chickie pushed close

Against you, between your legs and unzipped your jeans,
While in your head you heard your dad calling you home,

And Chickie into your pants. Once Mr. Quinones smelled smoke
On Chickie's clothes, said "Chickie, are you hot stuff?" Chickie

Promised he'd never forget Mr. Q. who held his cigarette
Between his middle and fourth fingers in the teacher's lunchroom.

But promises don't have the staying power they might have had,
The war's made people say things they never said, although to
    your mother

That's in part from your dad being gone, your being 17.
"Pudendum," you told Chickie. You made him say it, "not pussy,

Not twat." "Something that *must be* touched," he said, "from
    the Latin,
Like memorandum." Again the nuns climbed into it. By ninth
    grade

Smoking came easy and all the girls went ga-ga over Chickie
And especially over his brother Eddie who serves in the Pacific

Loading ammo. You have your war stories. Mr. Coler, who's
    German,
Had to go downtown with the Feds, and Mrs. Coler nonstop
    gabbed

How they arrived here at 15 and would never leave, and so on.
You tried to replay sitting in Chickie's living room,

The baseball game on, and his mom and dad pouring beer,
Listening, and Chickie pitching the ball. "Come on, sit down,"

They roared. Then the Yanks lost. Choretime for Chickie,
So you flipped through *Esquire*, which didn't come to your house,

Read the watch ads and saw women with darkly outlined breasts
Smiling at you, a smile you practiced in the mirror as you pulled

Your sweater tight against your bosom. "What a pair," the soda
    jerk
At Claremont Drugs said. "Screw you eggcream," you hissed back.

Sometimes you just wanted your body left alone.
Vagina, as if there were some genesis in yourself, you made him

Say it, "vagina, not cunt." Chickie said what you wanted.
Now his brother Eddie was packing his bag, leaving for San Diego.

Eddie, folding a white T-shirt, came in to tell you, "Wait for me."
This was news to you, that he'd be back for you. His mother
    cooked,

His father napped, and Eddie sat beside you, took the *Esquire*
    away,
Caught you under his kiss, like he was begging, like he knew
    what to do.

"My brother's a fool, a kid. You're the hottest dish on the block,
Or in America," he tongued and pinched you. "My brother
    doesn't know

How to treat you," Eddie said. He said your name, "Benita. You
    knock me
Out of this world, you're a beauty." His duffel bag was packed,
    his mother

Baking brownies. You could smell them. He said he wanted to
    smell
Every part of you, he really meant it. Later that night

You thought of him, and had your body to yourself, like a military
Secret. You don't often think of this, mostly sewing with Gloria

After school or doing errands for your dad who's in Seattle
To weld wings and might join up. You've got twelfth-grade math,

English, "the world's greatest culture," Mrs. Herlihy croons,
Teary-eyed over Shakespeare and Tennyson. You sit all hours

For Mrs. Gansvort's kid, she's named him Jesus, "A baby to
    grow up
During war needs a good name," she says. Mrs. Gansvort's in
    munitions,

Claims her husband's a bum with a supply unit in Texas, living
With a whore. She's let you in on this, lets you use the phone.

You say "whore" over the phone, wonder can you sneak in guys
When she's pulling overtime. On Saturdays when they're out
    whacking

The ball and it looks like more will go to war you think of who's
Touched you, where they are, how quiet it might be,

Then you tell yourself loose lips sink ships, don't talk
Of soldiering, don't name what they do, what they may tell you.

The Milkweed Parables

We bear the seeds of our return forever,
the flowers of our leaving, fruit of flight . . .
MURIEL RUKEYSER

I. THE KEEPER

I

The girl saw something like it in the eyes of the men as they
    discussed how best to stack straw or butcher hogs.
Silently stirring the lard kettle with the heavy paddle, she would
    watch them argue about seasoning the sausage, then later,
    alone in the woods, try to wrinkle her nose like Augie
    Ochslein as if to interrupt her uncle, *Nein—Kein garlic!*
    Oskar, du weisst—no garlic in mine.
The others would laugh at him, but Mr. Ochslein clearly took
    pride in being the most persnickety neighbor.

Turning over leaves to find the new ginger shoots, she knew no
    adult would have appreciated such a finickiness in her, unless
    it was applied to swishing the bluebottles away from the
    cooling mincemeat pies.
So her vision grew in her eyes and her fingertips, and was called
    out at evening when the crows gathered along the opposite
    bluff of the creek.
And she said to no one but herself, *Tomorrow the hickory buds*
    will open their small hands and call down rain.

2

A demon of willfulness had once almost come to life before her in the coal-oil flicker of the parlor, as her uncle read in the almanac the story of a young girl struck down and disgraced by adventure.

And so she had willingly memorized the verses from the German Bible and stayed away for a month from the catfish hole in the creek and fence posts and other places where it would have been easy for the Devil to reach up from Hell and grab her.

But even then, she knew that she was drawn to another side, though she did not know what was there.

Even her breathing became less girl-like at age twelve, with her turning to walk up the small twisting draws from McGee Creek, watching the growth of the gooseberry leaves, the sprouting acorns where a tree had fallen, arriving home from school so late they assumed she visited Elsbeth.

And so she said she did and made up a story of what the old midwife had asked, something about *her boy, Oskar,* that made her uncle shift, then smile and forget about more scolding.

She only visited Elsbeth that next week to try to get her to talk about the same things as she herself had told, so that the old woman might later remember and reply about such a visit from the girl once that spring.

She had never gone into the house of a woman who lived alone before, a house with no man and a messy table, and everywhere small piles of leaves and bark and paper.

As she followed hunched Elsbeth into the kitchen, she bumped her head on a low-hanging shock of herbs, and white-plumed seeds fell from narrow pods catching like snowflakes in her auburn hair.

Elsbeth laughed and told her about curing Uncle Oskar of pleurisy with the root of that same plant as they drank sassafras tea and the girl only played at removing the seeds from her hair, admiring the way they glistened there, with Elsbeth's small looking glass.

3

Thus one called may find a mentor.

But there was only that one summer, after she had turned twelve,
when she lived with and worked for Elsbeth, as they both
told her mother and uncle, Elsbeth paying for the girl's *house-
keeping* with paper bundles of cures and a mixture for brew-
ing tonic for Oskar's mare.

It meant something coming in and nothing more going out to the
school next fall, except for Cousin Gus, Oskar's boy; it meant
a *hardworking,* more marriageable daughter for her mother.

But for herself, it meant finding Elsbeth's light in her own hands,
feeling the difference between poison and cure, as if in the
dark, for it was surely darkness that hid this light from
others.

It meant knowing, as surely as knowing straw, or butchering, or
burning brick or charcoal, and it meant laughing out loud
sitting at the dirty table with Elsbeth or calling in the crows
together from the shade of the hickory grove.

When Elsbeth caught the palsy in October's early freeze and
could not tell her what herbs to brew, she tried to find them
on her own, but Elsbeth was taken in a wagon to town and
died.

She never knew if she could have saved her.

No one held her responsible, but they interrogated her, asking
why she wanted to keep living in Elsbeth's cluttered house,
and for that matter, *how had* she spent her housekeeper's
time if the old woman's place was such a sty.

In less than a month, as Uncle Oskar returned to supper sweaty
and nervous, her mother muttered, *Fertig—Ganz fertig—
Ende,* and a fragrant smoke twisted above the hickories as
Elsbeth's herb stores burned.

The girl took up reading Psalms aloud each Sunday night and the
questions stopped.

But when Gus choked on a fish bone, the week before Christmas,
and she made him swallow bread, as anyone but a child knew
to do, Uncle Oskar blurted that God be praised that she had

stayed with Elsbeth, but then he glanced to heaven and down
again as if embarrassed and quickly went to see about the
calf.

Surely, the calf's small nose knew more about the light in yarrow
and in chicory and in maple twigs than her uncle, she
thought, but he believed his darkness was the light.

4

She learned to avert her eyes so that the others would not be trou-
bled by what showed through, and so she grew to adulthood
in two worlds, marrying Arnie Ochslein to please her mother,
who was ill, and moving back home to have her child when
Arnie was hospitalized with malaria in Manila, where he was
soldiering.

The influenza took her mother before the cancer and she passed
away in spring.

And when the government telegram came about Arnie, Uncle
Oskar pledged they would raise her baby as Gus's little
brother, while large tears streamed down both sides of his
furrowed nose.

Sunday afternoons that summer, when Gus had taken the wagon
to a friend's and when her Uncle Oskar napped as if beneath
the safe canopy of his pork-chop dinner, she would carry her
baby out across the farm, through the hickories and along the
creek, the small boy's hands mimicking her own as she
reached to touch the leaves or as she knelt to touch the water.

If she handed him a stalk of goatsbeard, he stared transfixed, and
he screamed beyond all decorum with delight when she blew
away the buoyant seeds.

And the wordless baby, like his mother, hid all trace of these dis-
coveries from the world of Oskar and Gus, kept it wrapped
within the pod of his small secret soul.

5

That Monday in September, she hadn't known the cow had
gotten down into the west ravine where the white snakeroot
grows; Oskar hadn't told her.

But when the new milk smelled strange, she had thought better to
    drink a little of it herself to test it before giving it to her child,
    and when it did not seem so bad, she drank a bit more.
By the time Oskar ran in to say that cow had trembles, the milk-
    sickness had already begun to double her over.
As she lay on the kitchen floor, she thought she saw her son
    growing into a boy; could that be him coming in with the
    doctor, she wondered.
But it was Gus.
The delirium's taking her . . . , the doctor's words floated apart
    from his bobbing face in the misty kitchen, . . . *the coma's
    next . . . takes a poison to fight a poison . . . arsenic . . . back,
    lad, . . . enough to kill a horse . . .*

She fought the pill, trying to push from deep within, as if she were
    again giving birth, but the last push seemed to heave her
    clear, beyond and above the house, far above poor Uncle
    Oskar rocking a baby in his arms and standing beside the
    doctor's carriage.
Her hands reaching at last into the top of the hickory grove, now
    she could count the weight of the kernels ripening before the
    frost.
She could hear the crows calling from the horizon, the echo of
    Elsbeth's laugh.
Far on the other knoll, across the creek, they seemed to be cover-
    ing something—baskets of new potatoes, she thought—in the
    kitchen of a farmhouse; a black carriage drove away,
    splashed through the ford, then kicked a small curl of yellow
    dust above the bramble patch at the turn toward town.

II. THE FLYER

I

In the black pool of McGee Creek, he touched his face, and it dis-
    solved in rings of light.
That game might have been at his young mother's urging, but he

had long abandoned such play when already the hired blade
of the dozer severed the meanders wreathing his lowland, to
shunt the current down a straight trough along the eastern
boundary of the farm.
And after the willows had been smacked smooth, as he had heard
the pioneers called it, and the old way of the creek graded
level, each corner of the new field lay quietly in the sun.

There was a year of gigantic corn.
But that triumph seemed a cheating when the next year floods
rotted the seeds, and the third autumn brought hail just
before the harvest.
He might not have cursed the roping clouds that day had he
known of the coming decade of dust, years when the
seedlings shot up as if to make a bounty, only to wither by
July.

At first he blamed the insidious milkweeds that also claimed his
field of sun.
For weeks he patrolled the furrows with his hoe, striking off their
milky heads, but still they rose by the thousands above the
dying corn, their seeds wrapped like snake scales within the
ovarian pods.
By November, their white hair shaken dry, they rose like a mist
above the bottomland with every breeze rattling the frayed
corn.
It seemed that the channel he had made worked too well, cutting
fast and deep, drawing down the water table as quickly as the
earth along the gully fell away from the foot of his corner
post.
Only stapled wire held him when the war came, and he was not
as sorry as some others for his calling up.

2

In every way, the training suited him.
His carbine seemed much lighter than the hoe, and his field pack
weighed no more from season to season.
He became a navigator in the Air Corps and watched the earth

fall away farther and farther beneath his straightedge and
   protractor, triangles gathering fields, woods, and seas.
On his vellum charts, Normandy itself looked no bigger than his
   farm, and the shadow of the bomber stirred glimmers on the
   Channel effortlessly as a child's hand swishing in a bucket, or
   a creek.

He felt blessed when his parachute opened out of the choking,
   black smoke of the plane.
But soon after the crash, clouds gathering from the North
   Atlantic obscured his bobbing face from the other flights he
   heard passing homeward overhead.
He cut the lines away but tried to keep one billow of the floating
   chute around his legs, in hopes it might hold a day's warmth
   within its white folds as night came on.
Suspended among the swells in his life preserver, he dreamt of
   tropic bays and jellyfish dangling their tentacles, always with
   a cold sloshing at his ear.

   3

Long after he stopped hearing the water, a voice came through
   static to enter his dream.
At times, it seemed as near and unending as his own slow but
   continuing breaths, unspooling through a modulation of
   grays he later guessed were days and nights.
The voice carried news of the war, invasions and lines held, but
   he tried to fix his mind on the smallest triumphs—a shepherd
   far to the north rescued by his dog from beneath an unex-
   ploded bomb—and the stories of human ingenuity that flow
   out of war.
A bounty, the voice told him, had been placed on the hollow hairs
   of milkweed, which could substitute in flotation vests for
   kapok fibers, now in short supply.
Children, let out of school in Canada, would collect carloads of
   the ripening pods for shipment to factories in Ohio.

A fever came on, or so he later believed, but at the time he knew

only that the space beneath his eyelids blazed up white.
He felt the bed drift away and the weight of his body fall again
    into the webbing of the harness looped at his crotch.
His head jerked sideways as the chute canted above him in the
    crossways gusts.

He had been walking a long time, carrying the crumpled silk, fol-
    lowing a furrow, marveling at its straightness and the fine
    texture of the clods drying brown along its ridge, when they
    took his arms and turned him around, bringing him into a
    corridor of brethren in white robes, dragging bandages.

He saw now that they had pulled him out of his coma and back
    into a world populated with human figures.
But when he tried to converse, the nurses only stared at his
    mouth, or nodded to one another, mumbling babble.
And his own voice dropped away when they led him to a mirror,
    and he saw, looking up from the comb placed in his hand, his
    hair disheveled, gone totally white.

                4

The ocean voyage, the bus trip, the VA hospital—the days ran
    together.
He longed to hear the confident voice of the war, rasping its
    reports of triumph.
He mused about his ancient bottomland field, the certainty of his
    plans, the care of their execution, the first year's bounty of
    corn.
When he awoke in the home, gazing through solarium windows
    across a broad creek valley, he believed for a moment his own
    will had transported him there.

Now even the seasons seemed to stream over him, the time punc-
    tuated only by the recurrent visits of a young hazel-eyed
    girl—a sister's child he told himself, though he remembered
    no sister, or a cousin's, if they had returned him to Mount
    Sterling.

The youngster became one known face in a room of empty stares,
and what he liked best was that she never tried to make him
speak.
Instead, the child would carefully turn his chair at evening so he
could watch the sun light up the serpentine coils of the creek
lying on the far side of the valley.
She seemed to detect in his eyes how this sight engaged him.

One evening, as the glint had just left the meanders and while the
salmon gold was fast receding on the trace of cirrus, he
glanced down to discover his niece, as he had come to think
of her, taking his left hand quietly in her own.
More to examine it than to show some pointless tenderness they
were both beyond, he adjudged looking on; *how they had
become such idle curiosities for one another.*

But as he watched, the dry flesh across his palm began to split,
falling open at her touch. Dozens of small umber faces, won-
derments trailing plumes of white hair, began erupting from
his lifeline.
Soon hundreds floated by their hair in the space around him.
Thousands obscured the child, the sun.

He felt his body lighten among them, as if he were adrift in the
endless white of a cool sea.

III. THE PASSENGER

I

Riding the train from Hyde Park, the cool morning of her fiftieth
birthday, she had imagined becoming one of the museum's
docents leading schoolkids through the cultural exhibits, but
as her group turned through a musty granite arch, they would
suddenly be outdoors, the children turned into Potawatomis
in black blankets welcoming DuSable—and behind a hut,

where pumpkins were being cut into rings for drying, a crowd
of Hungarian stockyard workers with their *women and
children and a keg of beer and an accordion.*
The train itself, then, emerged from a tunnel onto a crescent
mound of glacial moraine, passing ice blocks studded with
corpuscles of granite from the Canadian Shield, each bobbing
gently in one of the prairie potholes dotting the flats that
seemed to reach southwest all the way to Blue Island, where
the train slowed and an interesting-looking man she thought
she had noticed on the train another morning waved to her
from a wetland, mouthed *Hi, Honey,* yanked the cord of his
gasoline-powered trimmer, and roared a swath through the
swamp milkweeds.

On such days, when the train was quiet, each passenger as lulled
or as convoluted as she, she could lose track of her own state
of wakefulness, the city streaming by, itself a dream, the con-
ductor's voice calling stops from the mouth of a triumphant
statue in Grant Park, his gray index finger raised amid the
pink branches of trees, calling, calling to each fellow traveler.

It was just such a hand, monumentally old, that came and went in
her night dreams and night sweats, though not a hand
upraised in triumph, but one curled down like an old root,
the gray blanket, at first beneath it, changing to tan clay, like
the soil under her own tiny fingernails, her own hand sudden-
ly shrunken, pale, dimpled over the knuckles, a child's.
There would always be the shadow of a benign face, which
moments earlier had drawn her near, yet always her gaze
would seize upon the leathered knuckles, and she would
reach out to them, taking them up mildly, as if unafraid,
while elsewhere deep within her frozen body knowledge of
the impending destroyer's clasp hovered and churned, dash-
ing sour the warm milk she had sipped in vain.

There was never any avoiding of her dark fate.
It formed the very procession of her nights since childhood, and
with every reaching she again became a child, open-eyed,

innocently placing her hand into the trap of flesh, silent, warmed as if by unseen rays, loved even, until she tried to pull back.

The train was safer rest, she even took it on her day off, it was just the vehicle for the urban botanist, just the thing to break the spell of the museum's desiccated herbarium pages, cabinets of leaves and bark and paper.

True, she had no alternative; her only other wheels, the 1939 Ford 9-N tractor her father had purchased the day she was born, now rusted, some two hundred miles away, in a tumbled-down shed near McGee Creek, preserved for her in its natural coating of bird guano by the neighbor who bought the old homeplace years ago.

Unlike this birthright, the train never gathered dust; a silo of diversity, it rolled onward as surely as the purple loosestrife overtaking the wild onions in the ditch just west of the tracks.

2

What she liked best about working on her day off was the relaxation, the freedom to return to her favorite specimens of the Asclepiadaceae: the wax plant, the tropical carrion flower, and the native butterfly weed—orangest orange of the Illinois prairies.

As self-appointed volunteer-for-a-day, she could not be rushed or prodded.

Back off, or I'll go home, she once told a supervisor, and Ed, her friend, the black graphic artist, could hardly hold back his laughter—Ed, who loved the city enough to curse its inconsistencies; Ed, who could never understand the ones in her.

She had tried to make him see, the day he introduced her to fried egg on a bagel; she had tried to explain how the city, the suburbs, everything northeast of Joliet had all been the *Rat Race* in the language of her home near Stickney, where her family had moved in her childhood, her father, a little old for World War Two, finding his duty and dollars greener than corn as a worker in the Chicago-area defense plants.

Real home was the eroded, tan banks of McGee Creek; she had

learned to say *creek*, not *crick*, and *w-AH-sh*, not *worsh*, in
the suburban kindergarten.

Do you mean Honkies have to learn *to talk that way to get
respect, just like Black Folks?* Ed inquired.
*Eloise, you're just a victim of white-on-white-racism; they'll be
making you move into my neighborhood next if you don't
watch how you talk.*

From his baritone laugh and his nudging of her elbow to try
another bit of the bagel, she knew he had meant no insult,
more a trust, still she felt her love for him, like the failed fan-
tasies of past loves, withdraw inside her like a small hand, the
hand of a child, eager, wanting love, yet afraid of unspoken
punishment.
She hadn't opened her heart to him so much again.

At work, she and Ed were still *co-conspirators,* as he referred to
them, with her drafting plans and text for new botanical
exhibits, and him turning her notes and sketches into artwork
for interpretive signs and display-case backgrounds.
And today, feeling more cheered than usual as she cleared things
from her lab table, she discovered a note—in Ed's clear
draftsman's hand—attached to a parcel: *Air Corps flotation
vest: verify not filled with "weeds"—Military Museum.*

Weeds? The army is afraid of weeds?
As she unwrapped the faded yellow contraption, unclipping a
rusty D-ring, a dose of mildew spores rose from the speckled
canvas.
Wrinkling her nose, and trying not to breathe them in, she turned
up a seam, and began to pick at the threads with her dissec-
tion probe and scalpel.
As each thread snapped, threads as old as she, the point of the
blade rasped musically on the rough cloth.

Soon the handwork began to soothe her, letting her hum her way
back again into thought, into childhood.
She realized, calmly now, that there never had been a time when

she had been at home, now or then; on the trips to visit her
country cousins, she had never been one of them with her
citified talk and ways: she got into fights.

The closest connection came that autumn when she turned seven,
when her father was laid off from the plant for a time and
they had stayed on her uncle's farm.

The uncle, really her father's second cousin, hadn't lived on the
farm himself since before the war, had been shot down over
the Channel, shocked into silence, withering like a cabbage in
the nursing home window—surely no one to display along-
side the sabers at the military museum.

She recalled his wavering slate eyes and white-ash hair.

With the tip of her forceps, she withdrew a bright, downy struc-
ture from the vest's crumbly interior.

Milkweed coma, she said, raising the specimen up to Ed, who had
just returned with a cup of coffee.

I knew you'd know! he exhaled over the brew; *may as well throw
it out, though; they don't want to know the truth about
weeds.*

She couldn't help smiling, wondering at Ed's faith in her and at
her own knack for taxonomy—where had it come from?

Her uncle's mother, it had been said, was a bit of an herbalist, but
not a great one, having died of milksickness like Lincoln's
mother.

3

She placed the delicate white strands under the microscope and
focused.

A small dark fleck that had looked like a granule of soil at first
resolved into a short, barbed shaft—a bit of insect foot.

But then, seemingly without her adjustment of the wheel, the
image suddenly blurred, distorting as it did into something
gripping, shriveled, branching down.

She shuddered back into the cold backrest of her stool.

What had she seen, or felt?

It had almost been as if something inside her, some pattern long
    preserved in the onyx tree of her spine, had deformed like
    magma in the focused beam above the lens.

Gritting her teeth, she brought her left eye back to the scope,
    reminding herself to keep her right eye open.
With her fingertips, she adjusted the aperture below the micro-
    scope stage—no mistake now.
Here it was, clear this time, the gnarled, remnant clasp from a
    pollinium, the saddlebag of pollen that the milkweed shackles
    onto unwary travelers.

She breathed in, exhaling slowly to steady herself.
She imagined the Lilliputian drama, the small wasp kindly caress-
    ing the five-part flower, mild glee, or whatever passes for
    insect warmth, filling its thorax, until the fateful misstep.
How long did it buzz its voiceless scream before tearing free (or
    was it able)?
And even then, no complete freedom, still carrying the microbial
    baggage around for how many flights over the meadow,
    before finally implanting it in another flower, perhaps only to
    get trapped once more.

Bees have been found with more than twenty of these dried sou-
    venirs on their limbs, fated for capture again and again, vec-
    tors for designs beyond their ken.
How strange to find such an ephemeral flower part among the
    chaff of long-harvested fruits.

You say it's mine if I want it?

Ed nodded.

*Let's cross over to the lake, then, by the aquarium, and see if it
    still floats.*

4

Sitting along the breakwater, tying an umbilical of twine through
the D-ring of the ancient life preserver, which she had hastily
stapled back together, she felt warmed by Ed's readiness to go
along on their military field test.
He cheered her lariat-style launching of the yellow bundle and its
splash onto the green swells, where it bobbed and surged.
They sat a long while silently watching the vest, listening to the
faint voices that rode the wind from offshore boats, miracu-
lously pushing back the traffic noise only yards behind them.
My uncle was saved by one of these things—in the war, she said
finally.

What happened to him after that?

*They told me he died in the nursing home; I used to visit him
when I was a kid.*

They both looked out again into the blue distances of the lake.
Is gazing in parallel looking away? she wondered.
She could hear the breeze tapping Ed's shirtsleeve just above his
burnt-umber elbow.

Far out, she could see how the waves made band after precise
band of blue-gray and white, as if they were furrows freshly
plowed by the coal ship now threading the horizon.
Focusing her eyes more closely on the lines of waves, she imag-
ined what it would be like to float for hours or days among
them.

While she kept watch, the silvery ridges began to look increasing-
ly like the rails of the vast freight yard of a vaster but invisible
Chicago, and as the plane of the yard gradually tipped up
closer, it became a striated wall of ice, preparing to raze the
knolls of Illinois once more.

Intimacy Lessons

1

Above green grass clumps, coarse rusted wire,
bent steel fence posts, and heaped dirt, raspberry
vines curl stickery out of the windshield hole
of the dented hulk of a forties' Plymouth.
I hear the fearful springs of our father's
nineteen fifty-five Pontiac splashing
through the puddled ruts of winter.

2

Now is the time when the spiny frost begins
to melt off the tattered leaves of the curly dock.
By six-thirty, it will all be gone.
Is the leaf turned on edge? I am too close to see
except for faint rose veins over pale green ice.
Just now, my feet slip toward the white depth.

3

This pink rind of the year suspends all belief.
Starvation isn't working; only my will
gets thinner. The bird just under my breastbone
tries to get out, eats the suet from my ribs.

4

I dreamt the reoccurring dream again and waited
by the pond to find its heat. In the dream, when
the damselflies stirred the frogs, I followed
the cow trail through the grass to the opened
three-wire gate. I looked for the grass

that sprang instant from the broadcast seeds,
the square I scythed in the flowering spurge.

5

High water and wind blowing, low to the ground,
zinging through the hazel bushes, roiling over
fences, snapping cottonwood boughs, left a poplar
featherlike on the billboard for Maquon.
A broken cloud voice, the child in the green dress
weaves herself a headdress of red sumac leaves.

6

Many dawns pass unnoticed, but not this stroke
of orange on a stony range of clouds.
Once I ran from a cold tent to catch the sunrise
above Forbes Lake; the sun, forgetting
the height of the trees, was an hour late.

7

The turbid pool gnaws the coffee-colored bank.
What gems do you expect to find along
the sprawling hips of the Mississippi? God,
the bullhead swimming among dark willow roots!
I have started toward a shrine of sticks and mud,
the way toward tangle, where it all connects
like a pencil sketch, retraced studies of a face,
where the cosmos will cup its hand over me.

8

As the deerfly wears the fawn's spots on her wings,
so, in the damp shadow of eyes, dim retinas
become aerial views of rivers, wingprints of
mourning cloak butterflies, fantastic migrations
of starfish, sapphire stars glowing in the blue corn.
Such are the moist-earthed intentions, the politics of

morels, the last flash of red in the fall apple
twigs, the fragrance of a lover's unpinned hair,
the sad lover, so surprised to give up doubts.

Lowilva Letters

To hover two fathoms above the knee-high corn is the feat
    of my dreams these June nights.
                                You are there
        seated again beside me on the front seat of the Buick,
looking like the cover of the Penneys catalog, 1953.

    You unchanged, but I know the consequences, half of me
            surprised how calm we are, drenched in the cicada song
of our impromptu wings and the dank starlight of the floodplain,
as if we both had meant to fly from the curve on the Levee Road.

    We never land in my dream, and the band of willows
which must have cartwheeled us into the drainage ditch
    is nothing but a glimmer in the headlights' farthest reach.

    I alone crash, as the glare of eyes touches off the dawn
of your blood on my palms, waking me to thunder without rain.

And for the moment I'm convinced it is a message you have died
    in a distant state, some funeral home hairdresser brushing
back your hair to find what you have always hid, the white
    meandering trace across your forehead—my gift to you.

2

That day as children we climbed the river dunes
north of Oquawka—over and over, you always ahead
of me, the black Lab, Old Shirley, ahead of you.
You counted off each lap, I wheezed. The Lab
still ready to swim for the driftwood
we heaved into the channel, when I finally dropped

on the hot yellow sand, and you fell and kissed me.

We both were nine, both called the same man Father.
We had no name for who we were to each other, no name
for what we swam for, young retrievers caught in the current.

   3

A man of thirty who pats his belly and talks cute
to sell the sponsor's milk to the kiddies
can be a hit on TV, but he's a joke back home.
Arkey set up those shots of milk when I went in for a beer,
so I ordered my whiskey by the bottle like the black hats
in those cut-rate Western serials I introduced. You finally
said, *Get out, damn you.* We might have lived on together
in Buffalo Prairie after Dad died, the two of us
a natural family. I can't go by the house now
without thinking I've just missed you on the porch.

   4

You said, *Illinois is pregnant!*
                              Then who's
the father, I quipped, *Indiana?*
                              It was starting
even then. But mainly I hated you
wasting your time with that basketball player
when we could have driven to the river
in my Hudson. I told you he would dump you
when he got to college. And you were
never sorry, once we got there. As I brushed
the sand from my plate, you'd grab my face
in your hands, point my eyes up,
                              Look, Stupid,
at the clouds breaking over the bluffs, they're
doing it again! you'd say.
                              They're only clouds!
I had to say then, but now, at fifty, I see
it all the time: the lines of surf

in a billowing arc across the sky, mimicking
the great western bulge of the Mississippi
like maternity wear for the state.

5

I have taken to walking in cemeteries, among the lost
stones, without promise of perpetual care.

They are more numerous than morels,
waiting beneath rotted elm roots.

Pioneer settlers, infants lost to fever, families
cleaved by sleigh runners and spring floods.

I part a stand of big bluestem grass with my stick.
A marker appears, washed blank by a hundred years of rain.

I lift the small lichen-covered slab; words long dissolved
from the mud-stained side have left their imprint in the clay.

I trace them in reverse, close my eyes: *Beloved Sister.*

6

On my way to conduct the interview at the returning
astronaut's home, I wondered how I could rise above
the usual *hometown boy makes good* appeal. I was
on-task, professional down to my black shoes, dutiful
as my tape recorder, new batteries, tape already cued.

Then I saw *him* behind me in the rearview, him twenty
years dead, but driving a Ford through the middle
of Quincy—as if he were escorting me to work, worried
my alternator was going bad. Hardly looking ahead,
I probed the once-familiar hairline and twelve o'clock
shadow; only the ruby tip of his cigarette was absent.

Then I heard your voice, also years unknown, saying

Our father, softly, as when you played you were older.

7

What was our religion, anyway? Memory?
Penance? The family lore?
Or is that just another damnation?

What stories did we tell one another in our silences together?
I told you a story once that scared you away, west of the river, the
Firebird Country, you called it.
Away from the family touch.
Away from my Jim Beam youth that almost killed you.

There is no one here for me now, for my old age.
I would write you that I have changed, that I ask and expect
    nothing. But you won't answer; I have already written the
    answer on your flesh.
This is where our silence has taken us.
You are the pulling current in my blood, washing over the shoals I
    make of broken glass.

The Greenskeeper

In the spring and summer, Hank gets up every morning in the pitch dark, with his window wide open. His bedroom is filled with smells of trees, dew, and cool mown grass. It is before there is a car far away on the winding road, before the newspaper thuds on his front step, long before there is even a sign of life way up at the clubhouse. Hank showers, then shaves in front of the small oval mirror. He puts on his work shirt, pants, and still before the first hint of light, comes down to his kitchen where he makes a cup of coffee, packs his lunchbox, pours milk for the cat, opens the curtains, then takes his coffee out on the back step and sits there to put on his boots.

He is an older man, getting on toward seventy, though he doesn't really look it. In the light from his kitchen door, his face and hands are smooth and tan. His hair is white, but thick. As he stands again, he holds himself with grace and dignity, something old-fashioned, the way that men once stood on ballroom floors. He walks a little ways from the house, stops, and leans against a fence post. His coffee is rich and strong. There are stars in the sky. He hears the first rasping caw of grackles. He smells the still air, thick with pollen. And this, he knows, is his time of day—when the golf course lies before him, dark and calm; when only he can feel the pitch and roll of hills, how they slide toward streams, how the streams meander, the ponds fill and drain, how they freeze and melt, and with this morning's light will lie brimmed, glassy, and covered white with dogwood blossoms.

Peace. How odd. Yet this is what Hank has found here: this mild acceptance, this strange giving over of himself, like water smooth down a spillway. It is so hard to believe after all these years. After all the long nights, the crazed drives, vowing never to return to this small stony house, never to set foot on this golf course again. Yet always turning back, always pulling down his long gravel driveway, seeing the light above his front door, thinking *maybe, maybe.* . . . But finding the door still locked, no coat in the closet, no silk scarf on the back of the kitchen chair. Then climbing the familiar stairs, his hand firm on the railing, sliding into bed, the sheets cold, but the window open, the whir of cicadas, the slow throb way out at the pump house, the whole night pouring in through his window. And dew falling like gauze. Like peace.

And like a strange purity, he thinks now as he finishes his coffee, goes back to the house, snaps off the kitchen light, then begins his long walk in the dark, straight out, away from his house, toward the distant place in the blackness that he knows is the garage. The grass where he walks is smooth, cropped, and slicked with wetness. For almost forty years he has taken care of this—seeded, fertilized, aerated, mowed, raked, and watered. He has seen these fairways covered with leaves, frost, snow, turbid water, and dried sludge. He has walked to the garage in snowshoes, hip boots. He would swim if he had to. But this morning, like most, he feels beneath him that slight sponginess that makes him smile. He knows the grass is thick and green. He has done something well. It is almost as if he is getting somewhere, making progress, as if by mowing back and forth in wide swaths on rolling hillsides—as if through sheer maintenance or ministry—he might work his life clean and polished.

But even this makes him smile. Because Hank can see himself, his life, as from a short distance. He knows he can't change what's already done. He can't rearrange these stars, can't flatten these hills that rise and fall away as gentle as shoulders. He can only do his work, and wait. So he plants rows of seedlings and banks of azaleas. He wraps them for the winter in burlap. In the spring, he sprays for fungus and parasites. He cuts dead limbs from trees and paints the wounds with tarry creosote. It will never be enough, but still he does it. For it makes him feel what he yearns to feel. It keeps him alive—this angular man walking briskly through the darkness, buoyant, purposeful, his windbreaker swishing as his arms sway. He is like a commuter catching a train, he thinks, heading home with roses and chocolates, the evening paper. Except that the tissue of light that glows now is on the eastern horizon. It is dawn. And his home is behind him, a half mile away: a clump of trees, a split-rail fence, a narrow chimney against the sky.

He crosses a plank bridge over a marshy stream. He goes into a thick patch of cool mist and heads uphill, keeping his pace and keeping a straight line. All around him the world is greenish gray, the color of weathered copper. He sees shapes of bushes and trees, to his left a small elevated place, like a plateau, with a wooden bench, a wire wastebasket: the fourteenth tee. From farther away, he hears the Canadian geese, their plaintive honking, and he knows that soon, as the mist rises, they, too, will rise from the pond, their wide wings slapping the water. As he reaches the crest of the hill, he is almost there at the garage, though for the mist he can't make it out: the three big white doors for the truck and tractors, the gas pump, the sand pile, and, on the far end of the garage, the smaller door, like a bedroom door, with the worn brass knob that opens into his office.

How strange, he thinks, to see the stars above and not see the garage but a few hundred yards away. He veers around a putting green that is coated with dew. There is a small flagpole in the middle and sand traps all around it. He pauses to look at the tiny tracks of birds that curve and interlace on the surface of the green. Then, as he turns again toward the garage, he feels something odd—like a breath, a slight breeze in the tops of the trees, or something present in the mist that he can't quite discern. Perhaps there are deer again on the fifth fairway, grazing along the edge of the woods. Or perhaps one of his men has come in early and is waiting beside his office door. "Men" he calls them, though they are boys, really—all five of them, fresh out of high school, their ropy muscles, pimples, T-shirts and tight jeans. Kids with their first jobs. In love with machines, torque, horsepower. Their rolled-up sleeves and slicked-back hair. So hard, so tough. So vulnerable.

Hank shakes his head and laughs aloud. He sees himself as he was back then. Awkward and gangly. Gagging on cigarettes. Those hours in the mirror, his hair just right, his collar opened, his tie loose—dashing!—flung over his shoulder, like Lucky Lindy stepping out of a plane.

How can he not laugh and love this life? These cool, hard kids who call him "Pops." Their trumped-up stories about girls, "chicks," the curve of thighs, the slope of breasts they've never seen, or touched, or held. Hank is as sure of this as he is sure of anything. He sees the lie in their eyes, their hearts flinch, but he doesn't let on. As they tell their stories, he nods, smiles, claps them on the back. He feels their bony shoulders burdened with innocence. It is such a pity. But it is so wonderful. Sometimes, he swears, he could embrace these strange sons of other men. He could call them his own.

But no. He is walking on gravel now, the garage is in sight, and there is no one waiting beside his office door. He stops at the gas pump and opens the padlock that releases the handle. In the gravel there are oily puddles. A load of fresh topsoil stands to his left, the smell of worms in the damp air. He heads for the office door. Like any morning, he will go inside, reach up, and screw in the overhead bulb until it lights. He'll plug in his hot plate, make another cup of coffee, instant this time. Then he'll sit in his brown swivel chair, the casters grinding on the concrete floor. He'll spread the newspaper over his desk, check the sports, the local news, and pore over the weather map.

Yet Hank does none of this just now. Though he unlocks the office door, he stops for a moment with his hand on the knob. He turns his head and looks behind him where the mist still hangs like a veil. He sees the rectangular gas pump and the squat piles of sand and dirt. He sees where the gravel driveway leaves off and the grass begins. Farther away, he can even see his footprints as they lead back through the dew, down the hill, then fade into the grayness.

And it is at this point, where his steps disappear, where the mist and the ground become one—at a place like the edge of the world—it is there that he first sees her: an old woman in a dark overcoat. She holds her back straight, her chin up. She is standing still, looking out on the golf course, as if she can see something there. After a moment she turns, sees him, and carefully now he walks toward her. She doesn't move. She holds a neat leather purse in the crook of her arm. Her shoes are soaked with moisture. Her hair, he can see now, is silver, with strands of yellow, pulled back in a loose knot. Her face is worn, but not gaunt; her eyes tired and sleepless.

He stops about ten feet away. "Are you all right?" he asks.

"I don't know where I am," she says, whoever she is. "I've never seen this place before. I don't know what I'm doing here. Can you tell me how to get back on the Parkway?"

Her voice is thin and quavering, her face wide open, and yet she holds herself so calmly, dignified, her collar straight and starched, a silver brooch, earrings, her hands together, not even moving.

Perhaps she's crazy, he thinks. Or perhaps she's like anyone else, just something off-kilter: maybe a terrible dream, or a memory, the clock ticking all night on the bureau.

"Don't you want to sit down?" he asks. And something warm and protective flickers within him. It is an old, odd feeling, a tenderness that is very deep down. "Why don't you come into my office? There's a chair in there. I can draw you a map and show you your way home." He reaches out his hand as if to guide her, though something tells him not to approach. He turns and walks back toward the garage, and when he looks over his shoulder, she is following slowly, many yards back, nearly invisible in the mist.

He turns the knob and goes into his small, dim office. He screws in the light and waits as she comes to the door. He offers her his chair, yet she remains in the doorway, not inside or out, the knot at the back of her head lightly resting against the jamb. At his desk, he finds a pencil and a pad that says Agway Fertilizer across the top. He begins to draw routes and landmarks—he hasn't a clue as to how she has gotten this far out of the way.

"If you want to get back on the Parkway," he says, "follow the road here for three miles, go over the river, make another left at Nick's Stop 'N Shop, then follow the green and yellow signs." He wonders if she can tell that he is trying hard to keep his voice deep and even, as though this is all quite usual, this happens every day.

But she isn't even listening. She is somewhere else. She is staring at the far wall that is covered with pegboard, hooks, hanging ropes, chains, and grimy wrenches. She laughs softly, and for an instant Hank considers calling the police or the rescue squad—they would know what to do. But of course he can't bring himself to do that. It would be cruel, uncalled for. These things can happen to anyone, these things in the middle of the night. So instead he asks gently, "Can you hear me?"

Her face is soft in the light from the doorway. At some point, he thinks, she must have been very beautiful. She still is, though in a way that he can't put his finger on. Her skin is pale, lined, and loose beneath her chin. Her shoulders are rounded, though unbent.

"Would you like to use the phone?" he asks.

She shakes her head, no.

"Can I make you a cup of coffee?"

She shakes her head again.

"Well, I've drawn you a map. Are you sure you can drive?"

"Of course," she says, now turning toward him. "How do you think I got here?"

It is a mild reproach—perhaps not even intended—but still it hurts him, much more than it should. "I was only trying to help," he says.

She looks at the shelves above his desk, the piles of weather maps, his catalogs and ruffled pamphlets on seeding, liming, transplanting, mulching—helping things live, helping them grow. "I know," she says. "I'm sorry."

He tears the sheet off the pad. "If you get lost, give me a call." He writes his phone number on top of the sheet, then his name. Hank. "That's me," he says.

"I'm Margaret Perkins," she replies.

He nods, folds the sheet, and gives it to her. She puts it in her purse, and when she glances back at him, somehow he can't meet her eyes.

"Where's your car?" he asks.

She looks out the doorway where the mist has risen above the tops of the hills. "It's over there, beyond those trees. I can see the windshield."

"Can I give you a lift? There's a golf cart here."

"No," she says. "Thanks." Then she turns, and without looking back, walks straight across the driveway, past the gas pump, and onto the fairway that stretches toward the road and her car.

When she gets inside, he hears her start the engine, and sees the wipers move back and forth, clearing dew from the windshield. As he does every morning, he goes around to the side of the garage and picks up one of the long bamboo poles that flexes as he carries it on his shoulder. He walks out onto the golf course. It is a beautiful morning, everything green—not a deep forest green, but light, buoyant, yellowy now in the slanting light. The broad fairways roll to the horizon, dotted with pines, maples, arching willows, and here and there, the lush greens, fertilized, manicured, criss-crossed like checkerboards. On the bluff far off to the left stands the clubhouse, its shining mullioned windows, and below it, nestled among trees, his small stone cottage.

On the edge of the road, the woman's car still idles and hasn't moved. It seems to be waiting, like a taxi, or a cat in the shade. Hank is about to put down the pole, go up there and see if something is wrong, when the car pulls away, though not out of sight. So he continues walking, slowly and steadily. He doesn't mind if she watches. There is nothing he can hide: this is what he does, his life, his job, what he has been doing forever, it seems. So he goes from one green to another, stopping at each. He holds the thick end of the pole in both hands, waist high, and lets the far end, like a wisp, lay out flat on the ground. Then he sweeps each of the greens, rhythmically, evenly, turning his body with the long pole, making wide arcs on the smooth grass. He is sweeping off the night's dew.

■ Hank eats his lunch at his desk while his men are around the corner, in the garage, laughing and arguing. He is scanning the sports section beside his lunchbox, but his mind is wandering. He is thinking of the woman in the dark overcoat, with the silver hair—Margaret, she said. He imagines her driving, flying south along the Parkway, the road straight, no traffic, the miles whipping by, until she gets off at an exit—it could have been any exit—and drives until she runs into the fog.

How many times had he driven like this? How many times had he come to rest on some dirt road with the headlights off and the stars coming down? Did he really think there was another place in his life? Did he think he could drive somewhere else and be someone different? It seems so ridiculous to him now. So long ago. Yet he remembers its keen necessity: his whole body cold and jittery. Then getting into the car. Driving. The slow relief. Finally sitting there, emptied, the engine off and the windows open—having driven those miles just to run out of things to say.

"Isn't that right, Pops? You tell 'em!" It is one of his men,

"Diesel" they all call him, a wild eighteen-year-old with greased black hair, a self-proclaimed ladies' man, yelling from around the corner.

"What?" Hank asks.

"I say, you got to take them down slow—the babes. Right?"

"Whatever you say, Diesel. You're the expert."

Hank hears his men whooping and slapping their thighs. He smells them lighting up cigarettes and flipping the matches out on the driveway. He closes his lunchbox and leans back in his chair, his hands behind his head. Outside the air is hazy, early June, the sun beating down. This afternoon he will go out to the pump house and start up the sprinklers. If there's time, he'll get out the spreader and top-dress the greens. He'll have two of his men rake sand traps, another mow rough, two others cut around trees.

He is thinking of all this, the pleasure of planning, of keeping this land trim and green; he is almost nodding off, when suddenly—it is clear as day—he sees in the doorway a young woman. He sees her in profile in a frayed work shirt of his that is splattered with paint. She is resting, one knee raised, her back against the doorframe. Her arms are bare and freckled. Her hair is short, red, "bobbed," they called it then. She is slim, weary, lost in the big shirt; yet her face is flushed, vibrant, as fresh as a sapling.

It is Lois of course. So long ago. But she had never really stood in his office like that. It was somewhere else: in the doorway of their extra, "storage" bedroom upstairs in the cottage. She had just turned twenty-five, six years younger than he. They had been married then for a year. She was a sharp, energetic woman, restless when she had time on her hands. She read mysteries late into the night, rapidly flipping the pages. She threw herself into household projects, body and soul. And on that day, while he had been tending the golf course, she, without telling him, had moved all the luggage and empty boxes out of that small dormer bedroom down the hall from their own. Then she had gotten to work with rollers and brushes.

When he had come up the stairs after work that day, she was leaning in the doorway, the air glowing around her. Behind her the floor was covered with canvas drop cloths, rags, and paintbrushes. A stepladder stood in the middle. Lamps on extension cords blazed all over. The whole room seemed to hang with humidity, and the walls shone a creamy yellow, as soft as butter.

She was triumphant. "So what do you think?"

He stepped around her and into the room, his eyes squinting. "It's beautiful."

For a moment, she didn't say anything. The tails of the shirt hung down to her knees; flecks of paint were caught in the fine hairs on her arms. She breathed deeply. She stared at him, strange and serious, all alive with something he couldn't figure out. "It'll be the child's room," she said at last. "Don't you think it's about time?"

For over three years, then, they had tried. The doctors said don't worry. Be patient. Relax. But then one night—a Saturday, when he said that her bedside lamp was keeping him awake—she got up with her book and went down the hall to the room that she had painted. He heard her open the closet and pull out the roll-away bed. The next evening she went straight to that room, and a day later she hung her clothes in the closet there. He tried to talk with her about it, but there was little she could say. It wasn't his fault. It wasn't anyone's fault. She didn't know what she would do. She wouldn't even let him touch her—she couldn't help it. So every night when he came up for bed—after he'd heard the weather report and locked up the house—he'd pause by her closed door, see the slash of yellow beneath it, and hear the pages turning inside.

Now Hank stands quickly and walks to the small sink in the corner of his office where he washes his face and lets the cool water pour over his wrists. He hasn't thought of all this in a long time, or at least not in such detail: the way she had laid her book, tented, on her lap and put her face in her narrow hands. How he had tried to put his arms around her, but she had tensed, flung off the sheets—and then the sound of her steps almost running down the hall.

Drying his hands with a towel, he goes into the garage. His men are sitting on barrels and cinder blocks, their shiny black combs in their back pockets. They smell of cigarettes, bologna, clean sweat, and open air. With the towel, he snaps Wayne and Jeff lightly on the back. "Hop to!" They close their lunchboxes, get up, and he gives them their afternoon assignments. He stands in the wide doorway, hands on hips, as Diesel pulls away in the tractor, a gang of mowers trailing behind. Eddie and Jim take off in a golf cart clattering with rakes and shovels. Then the final two push rotary mowers across the fairways toward a stand of birches beyond the stream. They walk cocky, carefree, never once looking back. Their bare shoulders shine in the sun. Their shirts hang over their belts and sway like tails.

■ One of the things that Hank most likes is the feel of a summer storm coming on, when the day's work is done, the garage closed up, everything put away, when he has come up to his cottage to find the windows open, curtains billowing, when outside half the sky is clear, while to the west a line of clouds, dark as charcoal, is rolling in, the flags on the greens snapping straight out, leaves spinning, and in the air that smell: cold, galvanic, thunder on the way.

And it is at times like this that he goes up to his bedroom, crawls out the window and onto the roof where the wind is strong but the chimney is solid, where he smells that smell and feels it all coming: first hail, then a wall of rain, gusts, an instant of pure, white violence that seems so near, terrific. But it does not shake his house, or him.

Hank is sitting out on his slate roof, his back against the chimney, watching the clouds roll in, when he hears the phone ring through his bedroom window. He lets it ring and ring. It stops. Then it starts again, and he climbs back through his window, feet first, sliding carefully over the radiator. He sits in his straight-back chair with his work clothes folded over the top. He picks up the receiver. It is the woman, Margaret, on the line. She says that she is sorry to bother him, but she wants him to know that she had gotten home all right. She is very grateful for his directions, his patience. Then again, "I'm sorry to bother you."

"That's all right," Hank says, and for a time he is at a loss for words. A woman is apologizing to him, someone he doesn't even know, someone who hasn't even injured him, as injuries go.

"Well, thanks again." And after a moment she says, "If there's anything that I can do . . . "

He knows that he should say something, anything, now—if only to be polite, to keep the conversation going. He *wants* to say something: to tell her that he is glad that he could help, that it was all his pleasure, that if she ever drives down here again they could have a cup of coffee together. Still nothing comes, and on this stormy summer evening he is suddenly shivering, something cold and metallic at the back of his throat. Through his window, he sees the hail, like white marbles, bouncing on his roof. He smells the rain and thunder. He remembers her tired eyes, so bewildered, pained, and yet so strangely calm. He remembers the soft knot at the back of her head, and how the fine, loose hairs fell down. But then with so much regret—with so much still that he can't understand—he lets the receiver slide back in its cradle.

Now he walks out his bedroom door and down the narrow hallway with the guest-room door at the other end. He turns the knob, pushes the door open, and stands there once more with relief and horror. He sees the same buttery walls and the roll-away bed. He sees the crocheted bedspread and the dog-eared paperback on the nightstand. Though he doesn't go in, he knows that her blouses hang in the closet, that her socks, underwear, and scarves still lie neatly folded in the bureau drawers. Everything is there. He closes the door once more. It is painful, yet he has left everything just as it was—exactly as it was. Not because things can ever be as they were. But because there are things he must never forget.

■ Hank is sitting at his kitchen table beneath the flickering pale fluorescent light, composing a letter to Margaret. He has found her address in the phone book and her zip code in a pamphlet on the post office bulletin board. It is late at night. The faucet drips and the refrigerator hums. His cat, Juniper, is sprawled beside the yellow lined pad, watching as Hank tries to explain, in his small, neat handwriting, why two days ago he had hung up the phone.

Of course he can't altogether explain—he can't even explain it to himself. There are things he has done, or has failed to do, that simply do not make any sense. It can be only a moment, not intended or imagined, a mere instant in the span of life. But there it is—something grasped too hard or it slides from the hand—and a whole life is forever changed. . . .

Yet not lost or wholly wasted—this is what he has come to live by. A person can err, even unforgivably, and still redeem himself in some measure. A life can be of some good consequence. This he believes with all of his heart.

But Hank doesn't write any of this on the yellow lined pad. Instead, he makes a list of the jobs that he and his men will do tomorrow: he will sweep greens, they will change cups and mow tees and aprons. Then he tears the sheet off the pad, gets up, and tapes it on the back door where he will see it when he goes out in the early morning. Next he washes his dinner dishes, stacking them neatly in the rack. He takes off his boots and puts them, side by side, next to the door. He watches the late news, the weather, and locks up the house. At the foot of the stairs, though, he pauses, then returns to the kitchen and flicks on the light. On the pad he writes that he didn't mean to be rude. He didn't mean to put down the phone. What he wanted instead was to see her again. Perhaps they could meet somewhere. Perhaps they could talk.

■ It is your typical Howard Johnson's. Twenty-eight flavors of ice cream, all listed above the giant mirror behind the soda bar. Thick bacon cheeseburgers, patty melts, fries, even fresh garden salads, ooze in the orange light of the heat lamps. Great slabs of German chocolate cake lie like museum pieces on aluminum pedestals, sealed off from the world beneath plastic domes. The seats are of slick orange Naugahyde, the napkins crisply folded. In sky-blue script, it says on the paper place mats: "Your Garden State. Let's keep it that way!"

Hank sits in the corner booth beside a wide window looking across the parking lot and the southbound traffic streaming by on the Parkway. It has been years since he has sat in a Howard Johnson's like this, years since he has sat in any restaurant at all—except, of course, for the Nineteenth Tee, where on rainy days Terri, the waitress at the club, always serves him a beer and a sandwich free of charge. Some years ago, on Hank's sixtieth birthday, Mr. Davis, the owner of the club, had surprised him with an expenses-paid trip to Atlantic City: casino tickets, dinner reservations, the works. "Take a few days off," Mr. D had said. "Get away for a while. Live it up. You deserve it." So Hank had gone down there on a bus full of rollicking Kiwanis Club members. He had walked on the crowded beach with his shoes in his hands and his slacks rolled over his smooth white calves. In the mornings he watched the sun rise over the ocean; in the evenings he sat on a bench with carry-out food and the *Philadelphia Inquirer*. He never went into the casinos or used the dinner reservations. He returned a day earlier than planned, not because he was particularly bored or lonely, but because he had seen all that he wanted to see.

Now the waitress stands before him and asks if he wants to order. He says no, he'll wait; he is expecting "a friend." He says it with no anxiety, with none of that nervousness with which, just an hour before, he had nearly knocked over a lamp, the electric cords tangled, as he ironed his slacks and his white Oxford shirt. Somehow he feels soothed by this wide-hipped waitress, reassured by the pictures of malted milks on the menu and the voice of Sinatra wafting down from the little round speakers in the ceiling. It is almost as if the world had stopped here at this Howard Johnson's nearly four decades ago. Hank was barely thirty then, not even married. He wore wide-cuffed pants and drove a sleek Buick Dynaflow, his elbow out the window. Now it strikes him as miraculous that any of that world is left, that you can still order a "Deluxe Apple Pie à la Mode," that as long as there are clams, you can have them here every Friday night. "Fried to Perfection." All you can eat.

When Margaret comes in, led by the hostess, Hank stands in his crepe-soled shoes, his sleeves rolled just below his elbows. She waves to him from a distance. She is carrying the same purse, and again she has her hair pulled softly back, those few loose strands hanging down. But as she approaches, she seems altogether different from the woman he had met that day on the misty golf course. Her eyes are bright, darting around the restaurant. She wears a light yellow sweater with stylish shoulder pads, and when she slides into the seat opposite him, a thin green necklace sways from her neck. She seems so attractive, vivacious—and Hank isn't sure if he likes her this way. She extends her hand and he shakes it. She orders the tossed salad, he orders the pie, and almost immediately she is talking, nonstop, with irrepressible good cheer. From her wallet in her purse, she pulls out a thick plastic packet of photographs: her children and grandchildren, one after another, all smiling, posed, as urgently happy as Margaret is now.

Soon their orders arrive, Hank's pie listing in a thick puddle of ice cream. Margaret is describing her oldest son, a pediatrician in Los Angeles—"He was always so good with kids!"—when all at once, in mid-sentence, she stops. She closes her wallet and puts it back in her purse. She gazes off toward the soda bar, her hand lightly touching the base of her neck. In the afternoon light from the window, he sees the dark pouches below her eyes, the spark gone from her face, and something else filling it, something so suddenly old and beautiful.

"What a fool I must be," she says. "Blathering on like this."

"No. Not at all." He looks out the window where the sun is skating on the parking lot, where buses idle and kids are sitting on open tailgates with hot dogs and melting ice-cream cones. Beyond the streaming lanes of the Parkway, a hill of buttercups and ragged grasses curves away as it ascends, where he can't quite see the top.

Margaret fools with the corner of her place mat. Then after a moment she says, "You know, my daughter looks at me sometimes like I've lost my mind. She doesn't see how I can live without him, my husband that is. He died last year." She turns toward Hank and looks right at him. "You don't have any children, do you?"

He shakes his head. And though he knows exactly where this can lead—a few more questions, a pause, and then politely and firmly she'd say she'd better go, she must—still he says, "I had a wife once. Many years ago."

Now he sees Margaret's face change and her head tilt slightly to the side. In her eyes, he sees a question form, a whole series of questions that he can never answer.

But then Margaret does something simple and extraordinary. It is something he will never forget. She spreads her hands wide on the place mat. Then she takes in her breath, and, as she lets it out, she seems to lay all of her questions aside—not forever, but for now. Because it seems more important for them to hold themselves there. To be calm. To do nothing that could lead to regret. To just hold this moment—not altogether comfortable or complete, but pleasant enough, poised for a time, her hands like that, all splayed and gnarled, their knees almost touching beneath the table.

"Coffee?" she says.

And over cups of decaf they talk and watch the dusk come sifting down. On the highway the traffic thickens and slows; a car here and there has its parking lights on. It is a Sunday evening, sultry and hectic, the start of another summer. It is like all of New Jersey is driving home from the shore.

■ At the Tee Off dinner in mid-June, Hank is the hit of the party. He feels ridiculous in his rented black tie, tux, and patent-leather shoes. Yet there he is, standing at the microphone before all the members and the board of directors. He looks suave and lean with his pure white hair and thick eyebrows flying up at the corners. He holds a glass of champagne in his hand.

"To all of you," he declares, raising his glass up high. He pauses dramatically. "To all of you—that is, all of you who replace your divots!" They all laugh and say "Cheers!" Mr. Davis comes up and vigorously shakes his hand. He says to Hank and all those assembled, "The older you get, Hank, the better this golf course looks!" There is loud applause, heads nod. "So, on behalf of the board and all our members, I'd like to give you this in thanks for your forty years of service to the club. May there be many more!"

Hank unwraps the package that is the shape and almost the size of a window. It is an oil portrait of himself that he doesn't remember sitting for. It is a vague likeness, though it's him all right. He recognizes his poplin jacket and the third fairway, dog-leg left, in the distance beyond his shoulders. The tweed cap that he is wearing, though—he has never owned or seen it. Now he holds the painting so that everyone can admire it. It will hang, Mr. Davis says, in the Eagle Lounge, looking out over the golf course. Everyone stands and applauds, and they keep standing and applauding. It is an amazing moment, touching, and yet slightly scary somehow to Hank, as if there is something here that he can't quite trust. The hall is filled with sound. Terri has gone to the piano, and now they are all singing, "For he's a jolly good fellow. For he's a jolly good fellow. . . . Which nobody can deny!"

In his head Hank hears it over and over, as he climbs his stairs later that night, weary with champagne and claps on the back. He stops in the bathroom at the top of the stairs and brushes his teeth. He goes down the hall, passes his own bedroom, then at the end he opens the guest-room door. He goes in and shuts the door quietly behind him. He takes off his watch and ridiculous clothes. The air is still and moist. He doesn't turn on the light—he doesn't need to. For he knows it all by heart, by feel: the smooth, fluted edge of the bureau, the place where the bedspread tucks beneath the pillow, the starched sheets, the soft crush of bedsprings as he lays himself down, gently this time, gentle as morning snow on the fairways, everything white, pure, untracked.

These things he has done with his own bare hands, these

things he has touched and torn. In his mind's eye, he sees Lois now on this same roll-away bed, her slender body curled toward the wall. She holds her blue nightgown tight to her knees, her calves milky in the moonlight. He sees the shards of wood on the floor, and he feels the splintered jamb. It all seems impossible, yet it was he who had done this, he who had thrown himself through this door, the sound of it shattering around him.

Why? Because the slash of light was at the bottom of the door, the pages turning inside. Because the light had snapped off, and not a word. Because he had called her name, and not a word. He had cried her name, and not a word. *If you want to have children, we have to make children. You can't lock a man outside.*

Then the shards of wood were scattered before him. The window was open, the night washing in, her freckled calves in the light. Her shoulders were narrow; her back, like a blade, was curved against him, her face intent on the wall. Then her hand moved, and she pulled the crocheted spread neatly over her legs. There was skin beneath cloth, and bone beneath skin. There was the odor of grass, sweet and fermenting; the sprinklers turned and clicked. Though he knew it was wrong—it could never be—still his own hand moved in the moonlight. . . .

Afterward he had lifted himself from the roll-away bed, thrown on his clothes, gone down the stairs, and, without tying the laces, shoved on his boots. Then he had flown out the kitchen door. In the golf cart, he had sped through the wetness, silver spray all around him, until he had reached the pump house. There, in the dim light of his flashlight, with the roar of the pump and the pulsing water, he had held the big handle that turns the valve, so cold, so hard—iron. Then with both hands, he had turned and turned to shut it all down, to hear it taper away—that soft drip like a faucet.

But as he had driven back to his cottage, as he had come around the tall spruces and climbed the hillside, he had looked up and seen that light. It was almost like dawn, yet fiercer, a pure white light just over the rise. And before he had even reached the top, before he saw it all, he knew. The cottage was aglow. Every lamp, every bulb and floodlight blazing, every window gaping wide. The kitchen door was open, not a sound, not a breath. As he had come inside, he didn't call her name. He didn't run to the driveway and see the place where the car had been, or the red taillights fading. Instead, he had gone upstairs and into that room. It was as if nothing had happened there, or nothing again ever would. The floor was clean, the sheets changed. She had even made hospital corners, and there was the faint scent of bleach.

■ Perhaps because he had never seriously considered it, or never had felt the need, Hank is surprised at first by how easy it is to get away from the golf course for a while. He and Margaret begin going out together once or twice a week, usually late on Saturday or Sunday afternoons. They meet at the Hot Shoppe on Route 1 in Woodbridge. Margaret locks up her car, a shiny Chrysler, and gets into his, a red '68 Volvo that he has never been able to part with, an old clunker with rounded fenders, rust, and a passenger window that is stuck half open. They go out to Pittstown, where the land opens up and the back roads are dirt. They watch the Fourth of July fireworks over the Boonton Reservoir. In the car, Margaret speaks again of her children who live in St. Louis, Norfolk, and California. Hank describes his men on the golf course, their silly swaggering ways, how sometimes he thinks he knows them, though of course he really can't.

On a Sunday they take the Circle Line around Manhattan, and a week later, in the heat, they stand spellbound behind a chain-link fence, gazing up at the brown splendor of Passaic Falls. Quite matter-of-factly she tells him about her husband's death: the weeks in the hospital, a tube in his throat, the rhythmic lift and fall of his chest, his strange, cool hand in hers.

Hank looks at her, and in her worn face he sees the fragility of things, the uneasy balance, the giving way of thinnest membranes and the dark falling on the other side. Yet in that same face, in her soft gray eyes, he sees such hard resilience—even the joy of it. And now he wants nothing more than to hold her, to just hold her, nothing more or less.

He turns back to the falls. "Well, I guess this is our Niagara," he says, wiping mist from his face with his handkerchief.

She smiles. "Actually it's quite beautiful." Then, her hand through his arm, they turn and walk up the littered path. She slides back into his passenger seat, over the silver strips of duct tape there. "So where next?" she says.

■ It is during this period in July, however, that some odd things happen on the golf course—pure coincidences of course, though as they occur, almost one after another, they don't altogether feel that way to Hank. For starters, two of his men get poison ivy while trimming weeds along the woods, and they are out of work for a week. Then when one of them, Wayne, returns, his first job is to replace the battery in the pickup truck. This he does, though he installs it backward, hooking the hot leads to the negative terminal, frying the entire electrical system, the wires sizzling in a stinking cloud of white smoke. On top of this come five days of solid rain, followed by the annual father-and-son weekend tournament, and Hank is behind in his mowing schedule. So he postpones for a week his next outing with Margaret. Each day he works frantically until nightfall, skipping his dinners, mowing the tees, aprons, and greens—triple-mowing, first with the grain, then against it, then finally on the diagonal.

By the next Saturday, he has everything mowed and back on schedule. In the late afternoon, he leaves a few sprinklers going where two weeks before he had reseeded a patch of the twelfth fairway—the fragile seedlings, like fine hair, just emerging now from the soil. Then he drives to meet Margaret at the Hot Shoppe in Woodbridge. They have dinner, they stroll through a park and, still warm with the remembrance of her hand in his arm, Hank returns home about ten that night. In his kitchen, he switches on the fluorescent light, goes out the back door, and now, in the golf cart, he is driving through the darkness toward the pump house where he will shut down the watering system.

He takes his usual route over the bridge, around the pond, steering clear of the ball-washer by the sixteenth tee. Approaching the twelfth fairway, he hears the familiar clicking of the sprinklers, though there is something strange in their sound, something softened and slowed; and beyond their sound is yet a stranger sound: a deep *whooshing*, almost a crashing, like the sound that a waterfall could make.

Along the edge of the fairway, then, he sees the four sprinklers, but they are turning slowly, barely clicking, so limp and pitiful in the starlight. The water pressure is low, something has happened, something has clogged or blown. Accelerating, he peers toward the deepening sound, and soon in the darkness he can make it out: a huge silvery column of water, a geyser, straight up, flowering at the top, as tall and wide as an oak.

In a second he knows it, and then he is there. The main pipe has burst and blown a ten-foot crater in the twelfth green. While he has been away, while he has been with Margaret, it has roared and roared, like something constrained and finally unleashed, shooting untold gallons into the sky. . . . Then falling and falling— the water flooding the green, the fairway, tearing deep, ragged gulches through his tender grass.

After he has driven to the pump house and shut off the water, he returns to the ravaged fairway. He gets out of the cart and walks around in a daze. It looks like a bomb has hit. Great chunks of sod have been thrown from the green. A birch is uprooted, the sand traps washed away. Everything tastes and smells of mud. It is sodden underfoot, his shoes squelch, though when he stops it is strangely quiet, strangely still. Then he hears a live thing rustle in a tree—what has he done or failed to do?—and the night, every-thing, seems to shake into tiny pieces.

■ Margaret has been invited to Los Angeles to visit her son and his family, and to celebrate her birthday, her sixty-third. On the phone she tells Hank that she's finally made her plane reservations; she will be away for three weeks beginning next Friday. He says he will miss her, which is true—absolutely. Yet he is also filled with a curious relief, as if during her absence he might catch his breath.

So while she is away Hank tries to live his usual life on the golf course. He sweeps the greens at dawn and gives his men their assignments. At noon he eats his lunch at his office desk, then returns to work; and in the evenings, at dusk, long after his men have peeled off in their cars, he locks up the garage and walks across the fairways toward his cottage on the hill.

Most of these days are spent repairing the sprinkling system and the twelfth green and fairway. In his hip boots, with the acety-lene torch in his hand and the steel-and-glass visor over his face, he welds a new seam in the ruptured pipe. Next he brings in truck-loads of sand and topsoil, and, using the backhoe, he digs out bunkers and fills in the crater and gulches. Alongside his men, he shovels and rakes. He works evenings and weekends; he'd work nights if he could. On the green he lays sod and sows bluegrass on the fairway, scattering the fine seed on the dark tilled soil, mulching it carefully with straw.

By the end of July, the heat and humidity have settled in, and his men are tanned to the color of walnut. On Friday afternoons, as they wait for quitting time, they sit on barrels and cinder blocks, all sweaty and tired with their paychecks tight in their fists. They listen as Diesel goes on and on about the girls he'll date; and then each Monday morning, seated on the same cinder blocks, they hear him recount his adventures—how far he has gotten, how he has "scored" with this girl or that.

One day Diesel arrives, proud and hungover, with a cigarette behind his ear and a small tattoo on his right arm: a leopard that moves when he flexes his bicep. "It drove Connie wild," he says, snapping his fingers. "I swear, that's what did the trick."

Later, as Diesel helps seed the twelfth fairway, Hank stops and looks at him hard. "You know, you'll have that on there forever," he tells him. "You'll have to live with that thing."

"Well, it's worth it," the boy replies, making the leopard crouch and leap. "You know that it's worth it. Don't you, Pops?"

By the middle of August, the rough has turned dry and brown. It hasn't rained for two weeks, and Hank has the sprinklers going full blast: the big pump sucking water from the river and, all over the golf course, those arching jets of spray, turning and clicking, twenty-four hours a day. One night he wakes up cold, shaking, his sheets all soaked and twisted. He finds the thermometer in the medicine cabinet, takes his temperature, but he has no fever. On his way back to bed, he stops at his window and pushes aside the curtains. He sees the sprinklers, frightening and beautiful, some fifteen or twenty, like a pod of whales, beached and writhing, spouting silver plumes in the moonlight.

He gets a phone call from Margaret toward the end of her trip. But it is a bad connection—and at midnight, waking him from precious sleep. In the excitement of her birthday, she has forgotten that she is in a different time zone, three hours earlier than him. She says she is having a wonderful time. Lots of presents. Sun. She's been to the Hollywood Bowl. In the background he hears kids playing and calling, "Grammy! Grammy! Look at this!" For a moment he hears her hand muffling the receiver as she says to someone other than him, "Hold on a second. I'll be right with you." Then he hears her hand slide off the receiver, and she is saying to him, "Let's see. Where were we?"

And he can't even begin to answer.

■ She calls him on the very day that she arrives home. She has just gotten in the door, she says, and maybe soon they can see each other. She could drive down to the golf course, if he'd like. She still has that map that he drew on the fertilizer pad. Does he remember?

Of course he does. Yet something inside him is reluctant to acknowledge it, reluctant almost to speak. He says, "Oh yes," as though surprised after scouring his memory. "Yes, I do remember."

Now she says she has something from California for him, a little thing, a souvenir. She insists on "dropping it off" this Sunday evening, as if she lives right around the corner. So he says all right, though she can't stay long—he has to get up early for work the next morning.

When she pulls down his driveway two days later, Hank meets her out on his front stoop. She is wearing a beige skirt with a narrow leather belt, and her skin looks darker than when he saw her last. Her purse hangs in the crook of her arm. In her hand is a small, gift-wrapped package with a bright red bow. When she holds it out, he accepts it, bowing slightly, then she follows him inside. They do not kiss or embrace. Beside the front door, he puts the gift on the table. There is an awkward silence. She is waiting for him to open the present, though for the life of him, he can't even ask her to sit down, to make herself comfortable in this place that is his.

Then, because it's so mild and an hour of light still remains in the sky, she asks if he'd take her on a tour of the golf course. She'd like him to show her around.

As they walk through his back door toward the golf cart by the fence, there is at least some relief in getting outside. It is a beautiful late-summer evening, everything amber in the setting sun. In the cart Hank pushes the accelerator, and in a moment they are gliding across the smooth fairways, her hair ruffling, Hank squinting, silent, leaning into the breeze.

When they finally stop, the crickets are chirping, it is dusk, and they are way out along the edge of the twelfth fairway. Hank parks the cart, and they step out on the grass. The sprinklers are going, the swallows diving; fireflies dodge and blink. To their left, the green is smooth and furled, molten, it seems, in the dimming light. The sand in the bunkers is white and clean, and on the cordoned-off fairway, the young shoots have arisen, a tender carpet of green.

She looks at the fairway, then looks at him. "Whatever happened here?" she asks.

So he tells her about the blown pipe, the geyser, and the deep rivers of mud. "It was while you and I were out together, right before you went away. While I was gone, all hell broke loose."

Margaret makes no immediate answer to this, though she turns her head slowly away.

Now he tells her how he and his men had worked overtime to repair it, how they had shoveled, raked, sodded, and seeded, mending this land for the past three weeks. "Of course it didn't happen *because* I was away, or because we. . . . " And he doesn't know what he is saying.

Yet he can see in the way that she keeps her head turned, in the way that she takes in her breath and lets her shoulders fall—he can see they have come to whatever they are getting to, that she has understood whatever he feels, that she has accepted it, sadly, and now, very soon, she must drive home.

In silence they speed toward the light in his kitchen window. Hank parks beside the fence, and as they get out of the cart, he offers Margaret his hand, but she doesn't seem to need it. In his kitchen, they pause beside the table, their eyes adjusting to the stark bluish light. Margaret picks up her purse, which she had left on the counter. Then they walk through the living room to his front door, still without saying a word. There she stops and suddenly asks if she can use his bathroom.

"It's at the top of the stairs," he says. And she climbs the narrow stairway.

While she is gone, he turns on the lamp beside the frayed living-room couch where his cat is curled on a pillow, and where he usually reads at night. He hears water running in the bathroom above. He hears it turned off, and soon he hears her open the bathroom door and step out into the hall, though strangely he doesn't hear her coming back down the stairs. Instead, there is a moment of quiet—just his breath and the droning crickets outside. Up there she seems to have paused, wavering, as though arrested by a vague intuition. Then he hears her steps again, but they are slow, cautious, and they are moving right above him in the wrong direction—toward the small room at the end of the hall.

For an instant, he has the urge to call her, or to run up there, take her by her shoulders and turn her around, forcibly if he must. But he is horrified by the thought, by the strength of his own grip. So he holds himself fixed and quiet in the living room. Above him, he hears her turn the knob of the guest-room door, and he hears the familiar creak as she pushes it open. He hears her take a step inside and flick the wall switch that turns on the lamp. Once more there is silence—breath and crickets. He imagines her seeing the ruffled book and roll-away bed, the things on the bureau: brush, mirror. He hears the light flicked off; he hears no more steps. He smells lavender faintly in paper-lined drawers.

Then he hears—he swears—Margaret calling his name. He listens, and again she calls his name. So he goes up the stairs, then down the hall. The door is half-closed, and he nudges it open. Nothing rips or shatters around him. He smells dew and grass; he hears the sprinklers. He sees in a pool of moonlight Margaret sitting on the edge of the bed, her purse on the spread right beside her. She has her knees together, her chin in her hands. For some reason, or for no reason, she has let down her hair, and she pushes it over her shoulders.

"What happened?" she says gently without looking up.

He looks at her, terrified; but she just waits without moving.

"What happened?" she says, and waits.

And so standing in that doorway, he tells her everything, in a voice of his own that he has never heard. While he speaks, she is quiet, calm; and when he has finished, she moves only her eyes. She looks up at him without amazement, without hate, and with something like love and deepest regret.

Now she takes her hands away from her chin and lays them for a moment on the crocheted spread. "I should be going," she says in a low voice. And he nods—it is all he can do—as she slides her arm through the strap of her purse.

She gets up from the bed, smooths the front of her dress, and slowly, sadly, she passes beside him, just moving the air, then goes out, leaving him alone in the moonlit room. He hears her walk down the hall, down the stairs, and pause for a moment before the front door. Then he hears her letting herself out and shutting the door behind her. He hears her heels outside on the flagstone walk, her car door open, close, the engine start, and the crunch of gravel as she drives away.

For a time he stands there in the quiet, still room. Then he goes out and into his own room where, without turning on the lamp or taking off his clothes, he lies down on his bed. He doesn't sleep, but neither does he lie awake. His breath is heavy, slow; his eyes are open. In the dim light, things go small, distant: the socks draped on the back of the chair—they seem to be miles away. He is thirsty, yet the thought of water revolts him. He feels strangely opened, hollowed, his skin a husk—any wind, any breath would take him away. But nothing comes, nothing fills him. The curtains hang limp before the window.

At some point he is aware that his cat has entered the room, has sprawled in the darkness, though he knows not where. At another point he realizes that the crickets have hushed, that the phone hasn't rung, the door hasn't opened, that a car has passed on the distant road without turning into his driveway.

Now he is jolted by the faint, new light in the curtains and the riotous sparrows in the eaves. In a half-hour it will be dawn, a Monday morning, and soon his men will drag themselves into the garage, then sit in a circle on barrels and cinder blocks. Though he hasn't been sleeping, he has gotten up late for the first time since he can remember. He has the sharp sense that he has missed something, something before the new light. He doesn't change his clothes, shower, or shave. He goes out of his room and is hurrying down the stairs, when he sees it—the gift—unmoved on the table. It is still wrapped in its bright gold foil with the red bow on top. It is still where he left it—where *she* must have seen it and left it—as she went out the front door last night.

In his hands it is light, a souvenir she called it, perhaps a trinket, a gag gift, like a miniature surfboard with a tiny thermometer in it—a small, wondrous offering. He holds it for a moment, turning it in his hands. It brings sudden tears to his eyes. Yet now he can't open it; he can't even hold it, and he sets it back on the table.

What is hers to give from the bottom of her heart he can't allow into his life.

He walks into the kitchen where quickly he pours a bowl of milk and puts it on the floor next to the radiator. From the hook, he gets his windbreaker and goes out the kitchen door. On the back step, he laces his boots. The golf cart is parked beside the fence, but he doesn't use it, even though it could get him to the garage more quickly. Instead, he walks as he walks every morning, steadily, purposefully, keeping his pace. Because somehow it seems more honest this way, to feel in his legs the ground beneath him, to know—or believe—that something is earned.

So he walks down the hillside and starts across the fairways, leaving his tracks in the dew. He goes over the plank bridge, then beside the pond he sees the geese sleeping with their heads tucked into their feathers. The days are getting shorter now, the mornings a little later, and within a few weeks—it is hard to believe—two of his men will go off to college, off to another life. He comes to the crest of the gentle rise where the garage is clearly in view. Yet now he keeps his eyes on the ground; he doesn't look up, because he fears what he will not see. He knows that Margaret will not be there in the mist, with her hair pulled loosely back. For this morning there is no mist, no fog, and the bright sun will soon be rising.

Perhaps, in the end, it is better this way. A life, alone, that he can hold in his hands. No secrets, surprises, or false impressions. What would Margaret think if she saw him like this? His hair disheveled. A gray, stubbly beard. And this same shirt that he wore last night: now wrinkled, damp with the cold sweat of an old man.

As he reaches the gravel driveway, he hears as from a dream a high-pitched wailing, a keening sound without any words, like the sound that a woman could make. It might be the geese, but they sleep by the pond. It could be the wind, but the breeze is soft. So he looks up, and what he sees is a slouched shape against his office door. It is one of his men. Diesel. He is seated beneath the brass doorknob, his head bowed between his knees. He seems like a lost child or someone who might be praying, so Hank approaches him slowly. The boy's dark muscled arms rest on his knees. He wears his usual jeans, boots, a pack of Camels in his T-shirt pocket. His shoulders are thick and wide. The leopard is crouching, black and bold, though the boy's whole body quakes. He is wailing into his big, brown hands, tears catching in the coarse hairs on his arms, then falling in splatters on the ground.

When at last the boy looks up, there is all of the shame there can be in a man. Something has gone wrong—everything wrong— and there are no words to say. The boy returns his face to the bowl of his hands, and Hank sits in the doorway beside him. He doesn't touch him, but he is there. He doesn't speak, but he is there. He sees the light splashed on the hills and soon in the tops of the oaks. He sees a car pass far away on the road. Then he stands and unlocks his office door, though neither he nor the boy goes in. Along the side of the garage Hank gets a bamboo pole and walks out toward the filmy greens. The morning is crisp and washed, pure and pitiless. With his shoulders swaying, he sweeps the first green, and on his way to the next, he stops. Before he turns around, he can actually feel it; before he sees, he knows. The boy has gone and gotten another pole, which bends as he carries it on his shoulder. His wailing has stopped, but his eyes are red. He is following at a distance in the damp, lush grass.

Beside the Passaic

It has never been easy living here beside the Passaic River. In late winter, when the snow melts and the rain falls, the river comes over the backyard, right up to the step. Once, I built a small levee along the bank with railroad ties and sandbags. It held for a while, but I learned: you can't stop water. It goes where it wants to. Every two years, it seems, we have a hundred-year flood. I remember one morning six months after I had gotten the job at the college and Claire and I had moved here. We were in our robes, eating breakfast and looking out the kitchen window. The yard was all water, except for the tops of bushes that stuck up here and there like islands. "Look, Sam. Look," Claire said, and I saw our picnic table floating downstream, its legs straight up in the air. We had made that table. I had sawed the redwood; she had sanded and stained it. Still, we had to laugh. You learn to live with this river. The next table we chained to the willow tree. It's out there right now—a little warped, weathered. I can see it when I lean back in my chair.

For almost five years, we have lived beside the river. We found the house through an ad in the *Star-Ledger*: a three-bedroom "handyman's special" with an "auxiliary apartment" off the end of the kitchen, an addition built years ago by the previous owner so that his aging father might live his last years with his family. The house was a bit more than we could afford, and clearly it needed attention. Some of the gray asbestos shingles had fallen off, revealing the tar paper beneath. Along the roof, the gutters sagged with years of dirt and matted leaves—grasses and maple seedlings had taken root there. Even so, we liked the feel of it, especially the half-acre lot with the dogwoods out front and the wide backyard that gently sloped toward the river.

That was the spring of 1980. We moved in the following August. In January 1981 our first daughter, Deborah, was born, and our second, Carrie, came along almost two years later—a year and a half ago. All the while, we have been renting the apartment to students, Claire has been working part time as an administrator at the county health clinic, and I have been teaching American history about a mile away at the college, one of the small state schools that are sprinkled throughout New Jersey. I don't have a fancy job. I am not on the "fast track," as it is called in academic circles. I am modestly paid. My students are so-so. I am here to teach rather than write books—and to tell the truth, it is better that way. Though Claire might disagree, at heart I am not a scholar. I spend more time in the yard than I do in the library. I don't work late into the night. I like nothing better than sitting here after dinner with Claire across the table. In the summer, the fireflies hover and blink in the backyard during the first hour after sundown. Later the moths bang against the screens and sometimes alight there, wavering, suspended as if by magic, so that we can see their feathery antennae, their muted colors, and the symmetry of their fragile wings.

At times like this, I can almost forget what the river is like in late winter. But of course, I can't really forget. On a Saturday a year ago last March, when the river was slow but rising, we were caught up in a strange current and swept through a narrow channel from which only now are we emerging.

Carrie was ten weeks old then. A friend had taken Claire and Debbie to see a puppet show at noon. I was sitting here in the kitchen. On the table before me, Carrie squirmed in the wicker basket, making her bubbling baby-sounds. With one hand, I rocked the basket, trying to make her sleep, while with the other I lifted midterm exams, one at a time, from a tall pile, corrected them, then dropped them onto the floor. The exams were horrible. Carrie cried, spat up milk. Her diaper stank. Outside it rained that cold, gritty rain that comes every March to New Jersey. So I thought about Florida. Sunshine. Spring training. The Grapefruit League. I hadn't seen a box score since October.

I remember taking Carrie from the basket and laying her on the table, where I peeled off her diaper and wiped her clean. "Such a cute little pain in the ass," I said, and tickled her fat sides until her legs wriggled and her mouth made that toothless oval that meant she would smile. "Am I right?" I dusted her with powder, put on the fresh diaper, snapped closed the safety pins—snug, not tight—I'm an old hand at this. "Snuggins, let's go get a newspaper." Then I buttoned her shirt and zipped her into her snowsuit, her arms sticking out like stiff little wings.

In the garage I set the basket, Carrie bundled inside, on the passenger seat of our Volkswagen. The engine shuddered and started. It was getting colder, the sleet icing the windshield, the wipers grating. I turned on the heat. We drove along the river, over the plank bridge into town, and parked in front of the pharmacy. I reached over to tuck in the blanket and wiped her nose with my hand. She was sleepy, her eyes heavy, the slow lift and fall of her chest. "I'll be back directly," I whispered. "In a flash." I pulled the hood of the snowsuit up and over her ears. They were huge ears, alarmingly huge for a child I thought. But "relax," Claire had said, smiling in that mild way of hers. "She'll grow into them. Just give her a chance."

Chocolate Easter rabbits, eggs, and jelly beans were already displayed in the pharmacy window. I looked at the back page of the *Daily News* and bought the *Times*. I talked with Norm, the druggist. I was only in there a few minutes. Five at the most.

But when I got back to the car. Well, the basket was right there on the seat, wedged between the passenger door and the hand brake. The blanket was tight around her. But her face: it was pale and posed, like an old-fashioned photograph; her skin a bluish white, the color of porcelain.

I remember a roaring sound in my ears. I remember picking her up by the shoulders and shaking her. I didn't think of it then. I wasn't thinking at all. I should have yelled for Norm, but instead I folded her into my coat, wrapped it around her, and drove to the hospital, holding her against me with one hand, steering and shifting with the other, running lights, swerving, fish-tailing, screaming through the windshield, as though I could make her come alive again.

I called Claire from the hospital, but she wasn't home. ("Pneumonia," the doctors had said. "It comes on quickly. You couldn't have known.") Later, when I walked out through the swinging doors of the emergency room, I slipped on the curb and turned my ankle. I hardly noticed it then. But even now it bothers me when I move it a certain way.

I don't remember much of the drive back. The river was as beautiful as I've ever seen it: the tall grass on the banks, the cat-tails, willows—all glazed, hanging down. And the water still and smooth. I wanted Claire to be home. I wanted to tell her, and I wanted to be with her. I think I wanted that more than I have wanted anything else in my life. When I went in the kitchen door, she was standing at the sink, sleeves rolled, her arms in the suds, her body long and graceful in the light from the window. Deb bounced in her highchair. On either hand she wore a puppet, and in the mouth of one, she held a spoon. Chocolate ice cream covered everything around her, including my exams.

"Where have you been?" Claire said, smiling and looking up from the dishes. "What's the matter?" Then, like a shade pulled down, I saw my own face in hers. I went to her, put my arms around her, caught her head in the curve of my neck. But she just stood still, her arms hanging down, the suds dripping off and pooling on the floor.

When I let her go and stepped away, she seemed a thing I didn't know. She wiped her hands on the dishcloth. She walked out of the kitchen, up the stairs, and through our bedroom. I heard her lock the bathroom door.

Debbie was staring at me, her eyes wide, then she started to cry. I lifted her from the highchair. She was warm and sticky; her hair smelled sweet. Holding her, I ran up the stairs and knocked on the bathroom door. I heard Claire drop her clothes on the floor inside, the shower running, the curtain pulled, her feet squeaking on the tub. I'm not sure that I said it aloud: She. Carrie. She seemed fine, sleeping. She was bundled up with her hood and mittens. . . .

But the door didn't open. With Deb in my arms, I sat on the edge of our bed to wait. The water ran in the bathroom. Sleet tapped on the bedroom window. In a few days, a week at the most, the river would be over the bank and cover the lawn with that brown foam on top. Debbie's sobbing slowed, and suddenly she was asleep. I laid her down in the middle of the bed and pulled the quilt over her shoulders. A moment later the water stopped in the bathroom.

I heard Claire step out of the shower and pull a towel off the rack. In her blue terry-cloth robe, she came through the door, her short hair combed back, shiny and black, her face sharp and refreshed. She looked at me with an expression I couldn't read. She sat beside me on the bed, her hands in her lap. She smelled clean.

"Tell me," she said. She wasn't demanding. Her voice was

calm—everything about her was calm. But I could see her on an edge, as though with one foot she were feeling the ground between us. It was as though we were back at the beginning, seeing each other. "Tell me," she said.

So I told her.

She asked me to tell her again.

I did.

And then we sat there, silent, not touching or looking at one another, the sleet still coming down outside, the steamy air from the bathroom, Debbie breathing quietly beside us.

"Sam," Claire said at last. She was right on that edge. "Sam, what are we to do?" And she didn't say any more. Instead, she rocked slowly, forward and back, rhythmically, steadily. I put my hand on the back of her neck. She let it stay, then leaned against it.

As I think of them now, the next several weeks were a frantic blur, both numb and tumultuous. For a time we all had the flu. The phone rang; neighbors brought casseroles. The river came over the bank, up the yard, and lapped at the bottom row of shingles on the back of the house. Often I'd find myself doing something quite ordinary, like vacuuming the hall, and suddenly it was impossible to do—I just couldn't. One afternoon two policemen in boots and helmets appeared at our kitchen door. They had an "evacuation notice," they said, "the river's too high." "Well, you have a hell of a nerve," Claire said, and she flew into such a rage that they retreated; they'd leave us alone. Then Claire curled herself in the corner of the living room sofa and wept for hours before she slept.

It was hard for us to gauge what we were feeling then. Claire was watching me carefully, I could tell, and I was doing the same with her. Sometimes I'd find her sitting out on the front stoop, looking at the dogwoods, and I'd stand in the doorway, searching for clues, as though by studying the back of her head and the slope of her narrow shoulders I might discover exactly what she felt. But I could only imagine her feeling my own sadness, my own upwellings of voiceless anger. We were encased, it seemed, each in our own grief. I think again of those willows along the river, glazed after an ice storm. They are still and silent, weighted with brittle hardness—a breath of air can bring them down. And so it seemed with Claire and me. We were terribly careful of one another. We barely touched. But still we watched and waited. While I stood in the doorway she would feel my presence, and without even turning around, she'd move slightly on the step, making enough room for me to sit down beside her.

We didn't talk about Carrie. Instead, by mid-April, we were trying to focus on living from one day to another. We made lists, went grocery shopping, and checked things off. We took Carrie's crib and changing table up to the attic. In her room, we scraped and painted the walls that had mildewed and peeled with the steam from the vaporizer. Meanwhile, Claire and I returned to our jobs after a two-week absence, and soon I got back to my chores around the yard. The river receded, inch by inch, leaving behind a broken shovel, a log, a tire, and everything layered and reeking with sludge. One day, as Claire was hanging out laundry, I raked the sludge in a long line across the lawn. The sun was warm, the river calm. The sludge was thick and had dried into a crisp brown crust that loosened in slabs. I raked it down to the river and whisked it over the bank, revealing the tender grass beneath. Claire and I were mending, it seemed.

But then there was that night in the river. It was June, when the evenings get warm and muggy. Carrie had been gone for three months, Debbie was spending a few days with Claire's parents at their cottage on Lake Hopatcong, and I had come home late from a committee meeting. As I came out of the garage, I saw a spot of orange light far away on the surface of the river. I stood, briefcase in hand, and watched it. It moved slowly downstream, stopped, and moved haltingly back up. It glowed for an instant, dimmed, then glowed again. Now and then it would disappear, itself eclipsed, but its light reflected on the water around it. I was going to call Claire out of the house, but somehow this was my own mystery. So I walked down toward the river, avoiding our seepage pit to my left. A small haze hovered above the orange spot, caught its light, then dissipated. It didn't move as I approached, just glowed and dimmed. When I reached the bank, I could make it out: in the middle of the river, a cigarette. And someone treading water to keep it there.

"Claire?" I couldn't see, but you feel these things.

The cigarette glowed.

"Claire?" The word hung, dissipated with the smoke. "Is it you? Are you all right?"

I remember the sound from the river: a laugh, a giddy, uncontrollable laugh from another time—from before we had moved here, before the children—when we had first met at a party, drunk, and she on the floor in a red sweater, laughing, tying my shoelaces together; and I, hobbling, hopping kangaroo-style.

"What are you doing?" I called across the water.

Again the laugh. Then silence, except for the crickets, the peepers in a bog downstream.

"Why, Sam, I'm smoking." Her voice—it *was* hers—had that old, odd teasing quality, as though she had a secret for me to unravel.

I felt like an idiot. "But, Claire, you don't smoke."

An ash dropped off the end of the cigarette, disappeared on the water.

"You're right, Sam." She was serious now. "There are lots of things I don't do. Like smoking, like walking naked across the lawn, like swimming in the dark." The cigarette fell to the water. Claire's head, her hair straight down, was a dark silhouette. "Come on."

"What?"

"Come on."

"In the river?"

"Sure."

"We have neighbors. They have children."

"Who cares?"

"But, Christ, there're things in there. Carp, catfish, polliwogs, snails—who knows? What if one gets in the wrong place?"

"Come on, Sam."

I stood there, where even at night the edge of the river is as clear, distinct as a boundary. Land. Water. Here a grassy blackness, there the rippling starlight. And still you can slide from one to the other as down a muddy bank, not sure of where the bank ends and the river begins, not sure of how or when or where you started sliding. Was it when I got out of the car? When I saw the orange light? When I turned toward the river instead of the house? Or was it now, as I thought of her smooth skin in the dark water?

As I took off my sport coat, unbuttoned my shirt, stripping right there on the bank? Or was it then, the next moment, when she laughed once more and I dove, her sound swallowed by the river?

The water was thick and warm, the feel of things growing, multiplying; things taking in, consuming, excreting. It clung in my hair, ran down my face, the smell and taste so bad—manure from farms upstream, the gypsum factory, spillage, runoff, everything—so bad, and yet so rich and so alive.

I swam to Claire in the middle of the river. She was smiling and serious, something wild, a little scary. We side-stroked, face to face, upstream, beyond our own property.

"Claire, this is lunacy," I said, though I kept on swimming.

"Oh baloney!" She splashed water.

We were working against the current, breathing through our words. In glimpses, I saw her white breasts beneath the water, her legs scissoring, hands cupped, arms reaching, pulling the river, then reaching for more. Since Carrie's death, sex had not even been an issue, a possibility. Yet here we were in the river.

"But think," I said, "just how do we do this? There are some real logistical difficulties here. Like us even getting near one another. That's crucial, you know."

We passed the swingset in the Rittwiggers' yard. Their dog barked from the porch.

"How?" I went on. "Tell me. There's nothing solid, fixed. Nothing here to hold onto."

We stopped.

"But ourselves," she said.

We drifted slowly downstream, coming awkwardly together, both of us treading water with our hands, her legs circling my waist, and Claire giggling, splashing, me catching her strange laughter, keeping that crazy balance.

And it was more, though, than sexual energy, I think—or at least I have come to think. There was a commitment in it, an intent, a kind of frenzied will. All of those impediments, qualms, reservations—the color of Carrie's skin, the stack of diapers in the bathroom closet, the twinge in my ankle—all of it was there, not drifted away, but coming down upon us now as water over falls. It was all there in that warm, rich water—the death of her—treading, kicking, rearing up, and rolling under.

And yet we couldn't do it. We couldn't keep that balance. As we tried to lock, Claire went under for a horrible moment, then came up, crying and choking. It was just no use. We separated. Claire swam downstream to our yard, crawled out of the water and up the bank beneath the willow tree. I followed. Shivering, she tied my shirt around her waist, then wrapped my jacket around her shoulders and hugged her arms across her chest, folding in upon herself. Without a word, she walked away toward the house, her thin legs gleaming in the moonlight, bits of grass clinging to her ankles.

I have thought about that night in the river many times since then, and still its meaning is not altogether clear. I am a history teacher, and I am supposed to make sense of past events. This one, however, is more difficult than most. Something was unleashed that night in both of us. As it seems to me now, we were hysterical for a time, and that hysteria—or our awareness of it—made our union both more compelling and yet strangely distasteful, all at the same time. As I crawled out of the river, I felt unclean—and not simply because of the fetid muck and water. After months of careful nurturing and mending, we had suddenly lost all care. We had let everything go. We had gone too far, had tried too much, too quickly, and now that fragile thing between us, a web of finest filament, had broken. Neither of us had wanted that to happen. And both of us knew that when you thought about it rationally, if you considered the pure physics of it, making love in a river, particularly the Passaic, was virtually impossible—it couldn't have been done. But still there was that sense of failure and separation, that lingering distaste, like a faint odor that fills a room. Nothing in our lives was overtly changed. We cleaned the house, worked in the yard, and shopped on Saturday mornings. In the evenings we sat after dinner, then went upstairs together. If anything, we were more affectionate then. At night we would lie in bed beneath a thin sheet, silent and sleepless, holding like lovers, feeling an immediate comfort, and then a deeper sadness. It was as though we were reaching across an invisible gulf. Our skins were like boundaries. The more we pressed them together, the more they would resist, and the more it recalled that night in the foul water when we pressed with all that was in us—only to fall apart.

■ Toward the end of that August I was in my office at school, getting ready before the start of the semester, when I noticed a young woman waiting outside my door. I asked her in, and she stood silently before me in a college T-shirt. She was a student of mine from the previous spring whose name, for the life of me, I couldn't remember. She had black hair, long and straight. Her eyes were dark brown, almond-shaped, and on her forehead, where she pulled back her hair, was a tiny scar, the shape of a crescent moon. I recalled that she had sat toward the back of my colonial American history class. Though she had always attended, she seldom raised her hand or contributed to class discussions. She always came and left on her own. She seemed apart from her peers, older perhaps, though not measurably so. She was one of those rare students—quiet, intelligent, and self-possessed—who without any fanfare would take things in and understand.

"You're Sarah Morrison, aren't you?" I said, her name suddenly coming to me. "Have a seat."

But she remained standing. "I'd like to rent your apartment," she said.

"How did you know it was available?" I asked. "I haven't even advertised it."

She glanced at me with her dark eyes. From her purse she pulled out a check and handed it to me. It was made out to "Professor Collins" for $150, exactly a month's rent, and signed "Sarah L. Morrison." "I hope it's OK," she said.

There was something vaguely amusing, attractive, too, in her combination of ease and determination. "Do you know what you're getting into?" I said. "It's not exactly a luxury apartment."

"I know," she said. "But it'll be fine for me."

That's how Sarah came to live with us that fall. The apartment into which she moved with a U-Haul full of odds and ends consists of three rooms: a central living and sleeping area with a door leading outside; a yellow-walled kitchen with an old Frigidaire, a sink, hot plate, no cupboards, and a window (like our own kitchen window) that looks over the backyard and down toward the river. On the end of the kitchen is a bathroom whose peculiar feature, other than its smallness, is a narrow door beside the toilet, which, if opened, leads up one step and into our own kitchen just beside the washing machine. The previous owner, evidently, was as lacking for funds as we are. The whole apartment seems slapped together. It is heated by an old rust-colored kerosene stove that stands in the corner of the central room. The walls are thin, the wiring inscrutable. Routinely—whenever the hot plate is on in conjunction with any other appliance—a fuse blows, darkening the entire apartment and, by some bit of electrical wizardry, our own bedroom upstairs in the main part of the house. Come winter, the pipes freeze in the bathroom unless the tap is left on. In March the kitchen floods: boots and sneakers float over the linoleum. No amount of scrubbing or Lysol will get out the smell of the river.

As Claire and I are not exactly the landlord types, there was no lease for Sarah to sign, no damage deposit. I showed her how to work the kerosene heater and replace the fuses. And to better insure her privacy (and restrain Debbie's wanderings), I blocked off the narrow door between our kitchen and the apartment bathroom with an old armchair. During the fall, it became a favorite place of Claire's, where often she'd sit alone, absorbed in a book or magazine, her legs curled beneath her.

For the first month Sarah was in our apartment, we hardly saw or heard from her. She never had company. Her telephone seldom rang. As far as I could tell, she rode her bike into school early in the mornings and returned sometime in the afternoons. We were all on different schedules, including Claire and me. "I need some time and space for myself," Claire had said. So on weekdays when she came back from the clinic at noon, I would take the car, drop Debbie at day care, and go into school to teach my afternoon classes. In the evenings, of course, Claire and I would be together. Since that night in the river, we hadn't made much progress. Despite our efforts and intentions, we seemed to be drifting farther apart. After Deb was in bed, we would sit here at the table and try to talk about what we were feeling. Yet somehow it was harder than we ever imagined. We would start out calmly, almost clinically. We might review what had happened in the last six months. We could say that it would take time to recover, that there were stages to go through. Then, somewhere along the line, we would strike a nerve. Through the screen door we'd catch the ripe scent of the river. Or in Claire's eyes I'd see a hopelessness that I had never seen before. Then we would sit in a silence that sometimes I just couldn't bear.

I would get up, go out the door and walk outside. There would be faint sounds of faraway traffic, the feel of loose gravel, the smell of damp, withered leaves along the sides of the dark road. When later I'd return to the house, the kitchen light would still be on, the door unlocked, but Claire would be upstairs, in bed, her head turned away toward the wall. As I'd slide in beside her, I could tell that she was wide awake, that while I had been out walking she had been lying there, filled with the same fears—and yet we could do nothing to share them.

On a cool Sunday afternoon in mid-October, I began putting up the storm windows. I took them out of the cellar, and as I carried them around to the side of the house, I saw Sarah hop on her bike and pedal off. She wore a gray sweatshirt, her wire bike baskets were stuffed with laundry, and when she went out the driveway, she turned and waved tentatively. Using the step ladder, I hung the windows, then went inside to hook them in at the sills. I started in Sarah's apartment.

I hadn't been in there since she had arrived. Though I knew she was out, it was strangely quiet—just the slow drip of the kitchen faucet, which someday soon I'll get around to fixing. I stood in the main room for a moment. Beneath the window was a brown convertible sofa that Claire and I had picked up at a garage sale years ago. There in the corner stood the kerosene heater, warm to the touch, and over the stovepipe hung a pair of white knee socks, worn at the heel. I leaned over the sofa and secured the storm window, pushing the metal hook through the screw eye in the sill. I went into the kitchen. The small formica table was covered with a red-checked cloth, and on it stood a vase filled with tasseled grasses that Sarah must have collected along the river. Beside that lay an open organic chemistry textbook, a pencil in the binding, underscored passages, and an entire page circled by cryptic formulae. I hooked in the storm window above the sink. Though there were no windows in the bathroom, I pushed open the door anyway and turned on the light. It was cool in there, the smell of mildew and sweet shampoo. A damp towel hung on the rack, and on the tiled floor of the shower lay a strand of long hair, black and gleaming.

It is hard to describe the effect of seeing these things. It wasn't mysterious or surprising. These were the everyday items of Sarah's life—a lost strand of hair, calico curtains, a crust of bread on a dish in the sink. And yet it was as though for the first time I could actually see her living here: getting up in the morning, opening the curtains, folding the sofabed, turning on the shower to heat up the bathroom. In the evenings she must have cooked her dinner on the hot plate, then eaten on her red-checked tablecloth. Perhaps, as she ate, she listened to the radio. Or perhaps she heard Claire and me talking in our kitchen on the other side of the wall. I know she stayed up late at night. When I returned from my long walks, I would see the beige light in her windows. She was probably reading a history assignment or wrestling with chemistry problems. When she got into bed, she must have read something lighter—flipped through a catalog, a magazine—until she was drowsy and reached up to turn off the lamp.

One day during the next week, when I put my fifty cents in the Coke machine in the faculty lounge, I got two Cokes for the price of one. As I returned to my office, I saw Sarah come out of the classroom across the hall. She was wearing a denim skirt and those white knee socks. On impulse I said, "I've got two of these things." I held up the Cokes. "A miracle. Want one?"

"Sure," she said, smiling.

I turned into my office and she followed. I sat at my desk with my bag lunch. "Have a seat," I said, and this time she sat.

I opened both Cokes and gave her one. She drank hers slowly, her books in her lap. I asked her how things were going and if there were any problems with the apartment.

"No," she said. "It's not as bad as you said it'd be."

"Well, you must be getting pretty handy with fuses in the dark."

She nodded, and we laughed a little. She looked around at my office: at the gray cinderblock walls, the maple outside my window, the filing cabinet, the disordered bookshelf, and on top of that the piles of paper, manila folders, and the small photograph that I probably should have removed. It was taken last Christmas by my father. It was of Debbie, Claire, Carrie, and me. Claire was smiling brightly. Awkwardly, I was holding Carrie, who was wrapped in a blanket, her ears sticking out. She was a month old then.

Sarah studied the photograph, and I watched a question form

in her face. She looked at me, and I saw it dissolve as she under-stood. I thought she still might ask, but she never did. Instead, we sat quietly finishing our Cokes.

Three or four days later, I heard a cautious knock on my office door, though I always leave it wide open. It was Sarah again. She didn't have anything particular to say, but I was glad to see her. Soon she began stopping by my office every day at noon, right after her class.

She would set her books on the windowsill and sit beside my desk with her hair fanned across the back of the leather chair. I knew she was our renter, a student, and only twenty years old; yet as we talked she seemed none of those to me. In her voice was a sympathy that I could not disbelieve. Without a word, she knew what had happened with Carrie, and she seemed to sense what was happening between Claire and me. Nothing was said directly, but somewhere in the course of our conversations, she made it known that her own parents had been through hard times, that for months they had lived together, virtually estranged.

Sarah grew up in Wrightstown, south of here, off the Turn-pike, where the land is flat, the earth rich, and the fields of corn and alfalfa go on for miles. Her father was in the military; her mother was a nurse. And I remember one day in my office when she talked all about cranberries. They are grown in the bogs near her home. Workers pick them in late summer, and along the sides of dirt roads, Sarah would watch the men loading them into wood-en crates with wide shovels. There were millions of them, like mar-bles, she said, shiny and red. You couldn't take what was in the crates, but what had spilled on the ground you could get by the bucketload. . . .

Often, long silences followed our bursts of conversation. Sarah would gaze out the window. As the breeze blew in the maple, shadows would dance on her lap, and I'd watch her small hands molding her skirt around her knees.

It has always puzzled me, my relationship with Sarah. Strictly speaking, it was not an affair. We never touched. I never so much as made an "improper advance"—nor did she. And yet, as we sat each day in the autumn light from my office window, I swear it was something like love. Anxiously I awaited her visits, and after she left, I went off and taught my classes with a strange exuberance that I hadn't felt in years. At home, however, she was as distant from me as she was from Claire. When I'd run into her in the yard, whether Claire and Debbie were there or not, Sarah would be friendly, but nothing more. As the semester went on and December rolled around, it seemed that this distance at home made our meetings at school increasingly intimate. In stages, Sarah opened her life before me, and I told her things that I hadn't told Claire in a long time.

When I'd return home in the evenings after picking up Debbie, I'd find Claire sitting in the armchair in front of the narrow door. She would have the lamp on beside her, a book in her lap, and it would strike me how little I actually knew of her life anymore. We were giving up, Claire and I. Without saying anything about it, we had abandoned our talks after dinner. Instead, Claire would return with her book to the armchair. In silence I'd finish washing the dishes, while through the wall I'd hear—or thought I heard—Sarah moving about in her own apartment, washing her dishes, drying her hands with the fringed dishcloth. Then I'd go into the living room to read the paper. Later I'd hear Claire switch off the kitchen light and slowly climb the stairs.

The first flurries came in mid-December, and along the edge of the river, a sheet of ice, thin as cellophane, inched out a little farther each morning, then melted away in the afternoon. As the semester was coming to a close, we got a cold snap, the likes of which we have never had before. It was a deceptive cold. The sky was clear. There was no snow, no wind. If you had looked out our kitchen window, you would have seen the willow limbs, yellowy in the sunlight, and beyond, the warm shades of brown and tan, the crisp shadows, the tall grasses along the river, motionless as a photograph. But had you gone outside and stood on the hard ground, you would have squinted in the bright stillness, smelled the brittle air, then felt the twinge in your fingers and toes, and the dull warmth that follows it.

It was during that cold snap that I came home early one evening, at dusk, before it was time to pick up Debbie. As I drove down the driveway I could see that our curtains were wide open, and there wasn't a light on in the entire house. I was struck with a sudden fear: our home looked abandoned, rushed out of—Claire had gone. When I went in the kitchen door, the armchair was empty, the lamp off; yet there was a dark and lingering warmth in the room: the smell of tea, cinnamon, the dim blue ring of the burner beneath the kettle. I went over to the armchair. It had been pushed aside a few feet, and behind it the narrow door was open. I almost went through it, but something stopped me. On the floor lay Claire's shoes, side by side. The chair I usually sit in at the table had been turned around to face the armchair. On the seat was a gold bracelet that I knew was Sarah's.

I was reaching to turn on the light, when I heard faint laughter, like children playing, from somewhere outside. I went out the door and stood in the middle of the backyard, listening. The air was cold and clear. My breath came out in white plumes. Already there were stars in the twilit sky. I looked across the lawn and down toward the river. It had frozen smooth and pale, clear to the other side. I heard the laughter again, and from behind the willow Claire and Sarah appeared. They were skating on the glassy surface. Claire held Sarah's arm as Sarah made tentative strides. She let go, and Sarah coasted off on her own, balancing, wavering, then flailing her arms and legs like someone in a Charlie Chaplin film. Claire tried to catch her before she fell, but together they went down in a heap on the ice, gently enough, their legs sprawled. They were like college girls off on a lark. Without noticing me, they unraveled themselves and sat there, looking at one another, shaking their heads, laughing.

And suddenly I knew: when Sarah left my office each afternoon, she came home to see Claire. While I was teaching, filled with that strange exuberance, they would be sitting in the kitchen, drinking their tea. Sarah would hold her cup in her lap, leaning back in my chair, her feet propped against the washing machine. Claire's shoes would be off, her legs folded beneath her in the armchair. Her face would be open, alive. They would talk softly and intently as steam curled up from the kettle and the dusk fell without them even noticing it.

I'm not sure just what I was feeling then. I thought of my own conversations with Sarah: her stories, her relaxed intimacy, the way she pushed back her hair, the bracelet sliding, then rested her slender arm on the edge of my desk and listened. There was something so pure about our meetings at school, so removed she seemed from my world at home. But now, to hear her laughter, to see her out on that river—and then to watch her, almost feel her, leaning on Claire as she righted herself. . . .

Sarah looked up to where I stood on the open lawn. I didn't know what to do. I turned to leave, but just then she called, "Sam." And the tone of her voice was as warm as it had always been in my office. I could see her there in the leather chair, her eyes wide with concern and sympathy. That was how she was looking at me now.

Claire's hand dropped from Sarah's arm, and she stared at me with a look of shock and disbelief. "My God," she said in a voice I had never heard.

I stood there silently. In the fields beyond the river, I could barely see the tall girdered towers that carry electric wires across the swamp and west toward Whippany. I had no idea what would ever become of us.

"Why don't we all go skating?" Sarah said, taking hold of the situation. She pointed at the wooden box of skates on the bank. "Yours are right here," she said to me. "Come on."

I looked at Claire, and for a moment I hesitated—was Sarah kidding?—but it was only a moment. There was really nothing else to do. I went down to the river, sat beside the box, took off my gloves, shoes, and laced on my old black hockey skates. The river was quiet, not even a rippling, an eddying sound. I stood on the ice, getting used to it, then dug in with one skate and glided off on the other, my ankle wobbling. Cautiously, we all skated back and forth along the bank, watching each other, keeping some distance, mingling without speaking, like awkward guests at a cocktail party. Then, as I was coming up alongside of her, Claire just stopped. Her face was expressionless. Her skates were white, the blades glinting. She wore her red wool sweater with intricate cables and diamond shapes. She seemed poised, waiting, as though listening to something far away.

Suddenly she skated swiftly off in a wide arc, upstream and toward the middle of the river. Sarah and I, yards apart, stopped and watched her in open admiration. It had been a long time since Claire had skated, yet she was as graceful as ever. There was nothing forced or erratic in her movements. Effortlessly she gained speed, then, keeping her momentum, turned and skated backward, weaving her legs, her scarf fluttering, her skates cutting long "S" marks in the ice. She glided between the willows and birches along the river's edge. She passed rushes, cattails, and alders, brownish gray in the waning light. I will never forget the way that she moved on that flat, polished river. It was almost as though she was dancing.

Years ago, I recalled, when we were still in grad school, Claire and I would skate alone in the hockey arena. We were twenty-seven then, married for a year. On Fridays, after midnight, we'd take a bottle of wine, and with our skates over our shoulders, we'd sneak into the pine trees behind the gym. With a twisted coat hanger, I'd open the back door to the locker rooms. We'd feel our way along the wet, tiled walls, through swinging doors, and into the vast arena, cool and dark, where the ice lay like black marble. I'd find the switch box and turn on the banks of lights that hummed with electricity. The bleachers were blue. Brilliant banners hung from the rafters. We sat on the ice, laced our skates, and drank right out of the bottle. Then we'd stand, uncertainly at first, and skate wildly about in that flood of brightness. It was like being in the Olympics, Claire said. She curtsied and waved to the imaginary crowd. We held hands, went fast, tried ridiculous jumps, turns, double-axles, and spilled all over the ice. When later we stopped, giddy and panting, we'd finish the bottle, and I'd see the beads of sweat above Claire's lip, her face flushed, the wisps of moist hair that clung to the back of her neck. Leaving through the locker room door, we'd feel the sudden chill of winter air. Once it had snowed while we were inside—a fine, light snow—and everything was dusted, clean and crystalline. As we walked along the quiet streets, we looked up at the whirling constellations and tried to name them. Our legs were tired. Claire smiled and slid her hand into my coat pocket where I held it tightly. We lived in a small, third-floor room where the bed folded out of the wall. We didn't have regular jobs. Our lives were uncertain, but it didn't matter. We went up the long flights of metal stairs, shut our door, and knocked snow from our feet. We hung our coats on the radiator, then lay in our clothes across the bed.

Beyond the Rittwiggers' yard, Claire had turned and was skating wearily toward home. I looked behind me, but Sarah was no longer on the ice. While I had been watching Claire, she had quietly climbed up on the bank and now was taking off her skates. In her face was a sadness—and something else that I can only describe as love. I wanted to go to her and comfort her, but in a way that I didn't know and don't quite yet understand, everything had changed. As she stood with her skates in her arms, I felt at the same time an intense intimacy and an intense detachment. I saw her as I have seen our neighbors in their lighted windows when I go out walking at night. In that square of yellow light, while they eat their dinners or watch TV, I see their private mannerisms, their unseen faces. I know them, but they are apart from me.

And so it was with Sarah. When she turned, I didn't call out to her. I just watched as she walked away toward the house, leaving her small footprints on the frosted lawn.

After she went into her apartment, I skated out to the middle of the river. Claire was coasting, closer now. As she moved, her body was utterly still, open, her head thrown back, her face looking up, her spine arched like a bent reed. In a slow circle, she glided around me.

■ It has been four months since then. Another semester is winding down; the river has long since crested, and there are blackbirds now in the green sedge along the banks. Sarah left at the end of December and moved back into the dorms. For both Claire and me, it feels as though a love affair has ended, amicably, without regret, but still with an awkwardness and a lingering sorrow. Now and then I run into Sarah on campus; and last week, as Claire and I were driving through town, we saw her and a friend parking their bikes in front of the pharmacy. I suppose we could have waved, or stopped and said hello; we might have invited her over for dinner. But Claire turned to me and said, "Let's not," and I agreed. So we went on without Sarah even seeing us. At the light we took a left and drove toward home.

Dressing the Dead

The pickled herring on the salad bar
brings it all back to my grandmother,
the legacy unraveling in her speech
from holds in her body, growths
in her fingers. She speaks of her
mother, who brought home fish still
struggling, wrapped in paper, stunned
flat on the counter with a deft flip
of her hammer. Remembers scales
that jumped like sparks, the knife
worn to a sliver of moon slipped
under gills, through skin slid
off like a silken sack, hiss
of root-beer kegs brewing in the basement,
the baking bread that lured in the poor
they deloused.   A *Cohen,* born to duties
of a priestess, she gave up her gambler
boyfriend for my great-grandfather,
learned to draw blood from meat,
dress out the dead.
                              In Hebrew the word
"you" contains all the letters
of the alphabet, symbols which stack up
the house of man.
                              My grandmother sneaks
a piece of herring from my plate, tells of many
nights she put her sisters to sleep, her
mother alone with the naked dead. Pink

children given up too early to polio
or typhus, women cleaved open to let
out their infants, fathers whose wives
stayed up crying, baking knishes,
kugel, *cholent,* and fish for mourners,
the long week of sitting.

                      In the synagogue
room empty except for a slab, lit
by sky-blue gaslight, her shadow bent over
a stiff man, dipping into private places
mapped by loving hands, the taut limbs,
vestigial webs between fingers,
caves of armpits, ridged bone, slack
skin, limp sex. For just one night
she had the right to touch what no
woman could. A splay-fingered bather
trapped in a net, struggled over the body,
could spit a single word at the sky.

                            Beyond
that point there is no knowable, Reshith,
the creative utterance, beginning
of all.

        Through the night's silence
to the hour of burial, she worked
slowly in lamplight until her shadow
skinned from the wall, funneled into lips
of the body, fingering over eyes, all-
consuming, blessing, cold.

                    The flame
like an oil torch, blackened the ceiling.
She teased brightness from hard skin, sheen
of splendor contained in a sound.

                     You who
have struck this void, and caused this
point to shine, who have sowed a seed
for its glory, as the silkworm encloses
itself, have made the word "house"
from "head."

          Then the shroud she wrapped

bestowed its layered blessing, over
and under, between the legs, around
the belly, arms, benedictive silk tucked
under shadow spread over skin, each
soft horizon returned to its speaker,
his head propped on pillows,
thin mouth stretched in thanks.
She waited for the sun, turned off
the gaslamp, palm clamped on his mouth,
two fingers over each eye, one creation
returning its breath to that first
darkness, the first mourner who sucked
effulgence from the lips of the dead,
tongue out at the stars, meaning,
in *you.*

     The words
"you," "the sky," cannot be separated,
are male and female
together.

       My grandmother holds my hand,
sips her coffee, tells me how she wanted
to dress her husband, to kiss his curves
once more, how his lips needed painting.
His fingers like claws to grasp. Not born
a priestess, she could not sack
his bones, their language, refuse
of creation, in cloth.

A Marriage

My Grandfather Louis was a butcher.
Meat was his medium.
My Grandmother Esther was religious.
She would not eat unkosher meat,
or have him, either.
She kept it up a year,
sea-salt crystals leaching blood
from tough, kosher steaks in the sink.
Days, her Bible sat open to Numbers.
Nights, his spotted apron hung on the door.
Evenings he brought home tenderloin, triangle,
rib eye, eye of round, T-bone, flank, skirt,
chuck, brisket, tongue, oxtail for soup,
and yellow marrow, quivering.
She would not eat,
or touch it,
or touch him, either.
That was her way,
the way of the Law.
All day he trimmed the fat,
kept his finger off the scales,
cut up the best Texas beef
shipped live from Chicago,
dull eyes closed
below his hammer,
skinner's knife
slipped between the hides.
All night he thought of ways
and words to break her,
until he weighed
what she brought home,

exposed the *shochet*,[*] "a cheat."
They ate lobster, Alaskan
crab, prawns, catfish,
spareribs, pigs' feet, bacon, rabbit,
and Florida shark steaks, quivering.
My grandfather was a butcher,
meat was his medium
until he bought a store.
One day he boxed his apron
and shelved it in the closet.
One day she closed her Bible
on his cleaver, marked her ending place.

[*] *shochet*: authorized slaughterer of animals according to kosher requirements.

In Her Kitchen

The creases in my father's mother's
  hand curl back, the lifeline
    of her palm pinned
      to the ball of her thumb,

a tiny pit engraved
  by knitting needles, tacks,
    and knives. Her
      blurring eyes

hover, pleading: eat.
  At the peak of morning,
    she grinds turkey thighs
      for hamburger, whips

egg whites for mayonnaise,
  her perfume garlic,
    dill, and pepper.
      So many

years of grandmotherly
  whispers, watermelon pickles
    in a low glass bowl, an apple peel coiling
      on the counter like a snake. Shhh,

she knows a secret: when to add a pinch
  of sage, when to waive
    the chicken foot.
      Look,

potato latkes, flour,
  spaghetti squash. A lump
    of sour cream floating in her blood-
      red borscht.

Bar Mitzvah at the Western Wall

The same old prayer at noon, a Yemenite
boy, with his rabbi and bearded father,
faces the scroll, stroking
parchment with his
hand.
　　　　At thirteen I too lifted the satin skirt,
palmed a swirl and rise of letters
on the breastplate, hand-scribed words,
memorized tropes guiding my
voice in song.
　　　　　　　Sweat forks down the boy's neck,
his rabbi looping leather
straps around his arm and head.
Inside the cut cubes of hide, two prayers
scroll into themselves,
male and female curl.
　　　　　　When I read, my mother
shrank, my father wept. I could not watch
them both at once.
　　　　　　　Women across the fence growl
gutturally, below language, his voice
chanting softly near their small circle.
Distended skin above a muscle,
the text swells.
　　　　　　I looked out
at the audience of men
and women, generations,
a helix waiting for my voice.
　　　　　　　This is the body of law:
the shalls and shall nots, vowels
wriggling toward speech, waiting to lock,
our mothers, our fathers,
the skin on our skin, all our lives
between these poles.

He puffs up inside me,
a full-grown man, our prayer tuned
to the cadence of all men.
                              The women whoop
above praise, ecstatic, hands rattling
the wire fence, no way through,
no common place,
no entrance.

The Clock

Earlier that day the clock stopped again. We had just replaced the batteries, but it was out again. The clock just hung on the wall. It was a cheap brass clock with spikes shooting out like a setting sun. In the middle of the circle, the black hands had moved around slowly. But it had stopped again, and Mama was tired of wasting batteries. He was dead anyway. That cheap Christmas clock he gave my parents was still on the wall. And the hands had jammed in place. At 2:14. I wondered if it was morning or evening and when my mother had decided to leave the dead battery in.

Sometimes, when I came home for Christmas, I thought to ask her to take it down. But then what? Do we throw it out? Put in another battery? Toss it on the heaped pile of basement junk? So it stayed, year after year, until it made an imprint on the wall and the gray outlines around the spikes left an abstract design.

They haven't painted that room since 1967 when I was in England and the riots started. I woke up to the London papers to see tanks flowing through the streets of my Motown home. People crouched behind mailboxes and fireplugs as the National Guard swept through, looking to pick off stray Negroes. Rickey got a rifle and rode the crosstown bus from the Eastside battleground to my tree-lined avenue. He came to protect them, he told my father. Sometime that summer, my parents became his. He sat in my mother's kitchen while she fried the chickens, and he filled up the buckets to wash my father's cars. That Christmas, I gave him a tie. He didn't have a suit, but I was giving all of my boyfriends ties to keep them equal and to keep from mixing up the gifts.

Rickey told me one summer that a girl had accused him of being her baby's father. "But she's not going to catch me," he bragged. "I know too many other guys to contradict it." He was proud. I was glad he wouldn't get into trouble. But, otherwise, I didn't care. I knew he loved me. He and my parents thought this virginity thing important, so I went along. It didn't much matter.

I didn't really want him to meet my friends. He was short, broad, and muscular. His long hair plastered to the side with a mix of Dixie Peach and Dippity Do. He was loud, vulgar, and yellow with a square Irish head. The first time I saw him, he was swinging across the auditorium stage on the curtain ropes. A boy that wild was a junior high school hero. I loved him with his Milk Dud eyes and his broad, fleshy palms, but he didn't fit in my life plan. He was too poor, too loud, too crude. His race impure.

I was excess baggage on the dance floor whenever a James Brown 45 started spinning. Rickey would jump, flip, and spin, and do the Detroit version. I think my friends began to suspect he was too white, and I backed away. But I couldn't escape him. Like a bad penny, he'd show up courting my mother and father and telling them about our future. He started his first paper route at 5:00 A.M. and was self-supporting by the time he was fifteen. I kept him in my life, and he burrowed in deep.

He didn't tell me he had enlisted until the day before he left. He brought me a Ken doll dressed like a Marine and a ring my mother kept. He liked the Marines. The pain felt good. They wore him until his body was sculpted like a granite statue of a Minoan man/bull. He bragged that half of them would die in Vietnam. So I should get used to the idea. I wasn't used to the idea that he was here, much less that he'd be somewhere else.

"I'm not worried about making a mistake," he'd say. "I'm worried about the guy behind me. The stupid, clumsy one that I can't see." The one he couldn't see who stepped on a mine and flew his fragments forward.

The war department sends neat, terse telegrams. "Killed in action. The date. Our regrets. Personal letter to follow." A short telegram to save tax dollars, but get you the news.

An early-morning telegram. I wanted to sleep, but the dorm mother insisted I come to her apartment. It's 7:00 A.M. on a Sunday—nothing could be that important. "Please come," she said. "Have a cup of tea. You can sit here if you wish, for a while." I folded the beige-yellow paper and replaced it in the envelope. "I have a French exam tomorrow," I said. "I'll be OK. Half of them die. It's expected."

I went back to my room, dressed, and spent the day studying. By evening, my dorm-mates knew, and we silently brushed our teeth in up-and-down movements. Sleepwalking through the rituals of grooming and studying. We never talked about it, and my grades began to rise. Exams, essays, all information stuck to my brain easily with soft, sticky glue. I could repeat back anything I'd heard or read, and the professors were impressed by my sudden improvement. The application of discipline, they thought. If only a student applies himself.

I dated him repeatedly after his death. In D.C. he was 6'4" and in Mexico he was 5'2". The Jamaican version showed up the year the wall was chiseled, and in Chicago he spoke with a Kentucky accent.

The clock is crooked and the spokes reveal the outline behind. I'd like to buy some new batteries, but the old ones are rusted in place.

Mothers: Three Stories

QUICKSAND

When my mother was ten, they took her mother away. One day a man in a white coat walked up the back stairs. Bottles rattling in his rack, he came up the unfamiliar steps one at a time. Grandmother Maggie peeked out of the window, pulling the curtain aside just enough for the corner of her eyeball to peer out. He was here, the man her husband had told her about, the man who would come and take her away to some dank hole of human feces and urine, away from her children, away from her front porch. She ran into the kitchen, grabbed her husband's hunting rifle, and burst onto the porch before he hit the top step. Pulling the trigger wildly, she sprayed the air with buckshot. "No one is going to take me to an asylum," she screamed. "Not without my babies."

The milk bottles flew into the air and landed on the cement, exploding like missiles. The man in the white coat ran back to the milk wagon. The horse, spooked by the commotion, bolted away.

When my mother came home from school, the house was strangely quiet. There was no noise of footsteps, no smell of dinner from the kitchen. Mother's baby sister lay in the cradle, sleeping easily and breathing with the long, full breaths of an infant. But there was more to the silence than lack of noise. There was a vacantness, a vacuum, as if someone or something had been sucked from space.

No one would tell her where her mother had gone. It didn't seem as if the adults really knew. Her father, a Pullman porter, had returned from a week-long train ride. Rolling back and forth across the country, shining shoes and shining his grin, he couldn't look after four children. Taking the express train to St. Petersburg, he tied up the children into four tight bundles and transported them to his mother.

Great-Grandmother Anna had a big steamer chest that she kept in the living room. Like Pandora's box, she never opened it, preferring to keep it sealed and safe. The trunk was so large that it filled half of the room. Blackened by age and mold, the hinges squeaked from the moist sticky air of the Florida swamp-fields. The tropical foliage that grew around the house grew within the chest. The secrets within were moldy, stale, and frightening.

Sometimes, late in the evening, she would open the trunk and pull out a few objects, photos with corners bent and pencil etchings faded and smeared. The images remained clear while the names grew smoky with time. My mother watched from the back room as Grandmother pulled out garments of animal skin, beaded and fringed, and feathers from some prehistoric bird stuck into hats and strips of animal hide. A few loose beads fell from the rotting twine and she rolled them around her palms, mixing the colors and shapes and meditating as if on a set of prayer beads. She looked up and saw my mother's face in the darkness. Grandmother was angry that the contents of her trunk had been seen by a youngster. Children have no business knowing about the past, suffering in the shame. They should be forced to move forward in time, forward in space.

But Pandora's box had been opened and fragments of bead and bone, feather and fur, had escaped and were flying about in the night air. "These were your people," she said to the little girl. "The Seminoles are gone now. Gone into the swamps, into the quicksand."

KOTEX

We lived above a store at the corner of Scotten and Milford. It was a quiet gentle corner and, from below, the ring of the cash register bell would fly up the stairs and tickle my earlobes. Penny candy was jammed into glass jars lined up along the edge of the old wooden counter. Canned goods were stacked irregularly on the shelves. Every few weeks, my mother would send me downstairs with a carefully folded note and a dollar bill. Sometimes I tried to pronounce the word *Kotex,* but it wasn't in my spelling book. I'd sit under the stairs in the dim light, tracing the word with my finger and sounding out the K and the X, practicing the word that came stiffly from my lips. Mr. Jones would read the note and reach for a long wooden stick. With an air of mystery, two metal fingers snapped at the end of the stick. He pulled a blue box from the top shelf, deep in the corner. He'd wrap it in brown paper and tape the corners down. This all was conducted with such solemnity and reverence that I stood very still and straight until the ritual was complete and the package was safely in my arms.

This whole mystery should have excited my curiosity, but it happened with too much regularity. I didn't think much of these monthly trips until I was about thirteen and the mystery became my own reality. Then we'd go to the corner store in pairs, my girl-friend and I, hand the clerk the tiny slip of paper with the word written on it, turn our backs, and pretend to buy penny candy and gum while he dragged the now-massive box from the top shelf. *Please don't drop it,* we prayed, as we saw the horror scene of a box of Kotex falling out of the grasp of the metal claw onto the head of the cutest guy in seventh grade. The box was double-bagged so that the name wouldn't show through, and we walked casually and quickly through the front door. It was hard to disguise the size and shape of that box as we picked our way through the crowd of young boys and old men hanging on the corner drinking from Coke bottles or small paper bags. Their stares and giggles chilled us even on a dog day. "These are for your mama," my girlfriend Stephanie shouted at them. Satisfied that she had bested them, we scurried across the street.

When we had five women menstruating, my mother decided that there were better bargains than the corner store. So she bought them by the case. A dozen dozen, which can only be called a gross. I'd hide in the shadow of a five-foot case of Kotex waiting for her to back up the station wagon so I could load them in.

■ "One day this wonderful thing will happen to you. You'll start to bleed and then you can have babies." Our Girl Scout leader was standing in front of us, beaming. This didn't sound like good news to me. I kept flipping through the pages of the booklet. "Every little girl wants to grow up to be a lovely lady." Okay, I could buy the concept. I'd shop for shoes at Chandler's, and wear itchy nylons, a tight bra, and a tight skirt. That part sounded fun. But I wasn't too sure about the baby business.

At dinner that night, I announced that I had decided to be an astronaut and skip marriage and babies. My daddy's limpid blue eyes turned gray, and he fixed them right on my throat.

"Well, Sandy," he began slowly, "that might be a little difficult. You see, you have to have a family because they only let normal people go into outer space."

The twins giggled. "They only send dogs and monkeys into space," one of them snickered.

I was determined to travel in space, and these small hurdles weren't going to stop me. So, when my small miracle began, I ignored it, then hid it, despised it and all the other signs of my approaching womanhood.

INTERIOR DECORATING

I graduated from high school and Bible school the same week with a diploma and a lily-white Bible with my name engraved in gold. They had prepared me for the world and set me out with a sword and a shield. After a few years, I started to drift back home. I couldn't admit it to my parents after the fanfare I'd made of leaving. So I frequented the seedier parts of town and partied with distinctly unbourgeois characters. I was free from the tidy, upwardly mobile, petty Negro bourgeoisie with edged lawns, bridge parties, and backyard barbecues, free of John and Doris's oppressive presence.

"Aren't you Doris Johnson's daughter?" a man asked me in a bar one night. "You look just like her. We went to grammar school together." The ashes from my cigarette flew into my eyes, and I started blinking wildly. "Didn't she marry Johnny Wilson?" he went on. "I think I remember that." He peered at me over a shot glass. I had never mastered the breathing coordination of cigarette smoking. I exhaled with the stick in my mouth and caused it to glow red and spew ashes into his face, too. "She's my mother," I admitted, and inwardly noted that this town wasn't big enough for the two of us.

She had always plumped up like a roasting hen whenever anyone said I looked like her. She took far too much pride in my accomplishments, as if somehow she were involved, and she continued to act as if we had something in common just because she had passed this face on to me. My mother was uneducated. She had finished high school, worked at a soda fountain, taken a few college courses, and started having babies. She tried working at the post office one Christmas, but complained that they expected too much accuracy. And she told endless stories about her soda jerk days: the height of her career.

Her silly giggling could be heard throughout the house, and she'd fry mounds of chicken so we all could have our favorite piece. She'd never do any dishes or housework and sewed countless ruffled dresses for her girls. All of my friends would sit in the kitchen and talk to her while she cooked. She fed them all and, eventually, every kid on the block made a daily stop at our porch door. "I don't know why we have to feed the neighborhood," I complained, and went to my bedroom to study. "Your mama's nice," they'd tell me in school. "You take her then," I snarled. I continued to study math so that I wouldn't end up in a ditch like her.

One day, a pack of girls followed me home from school. They started pulling my braids, and then kicked me. "You think you're cute just because your mother is the Girl Scout leader." God, now I was being punished for her sins.

So I studied and studied, making education the distance between us. The more degrees I earned, the more I could expand the crevice until it became a canyon she'd never be able to bridge. Our faces would be like two bridge piles on either side of the ravine with no way to come across.

When I turned thirty, I began to see her face creeping into my mirror and to hear her voice in my tape recorder. When I answered her phone, her friends would fall into conversations without knowing it was me. My shoulders and breasts began to broaden in that peculiar way that was Doris. My sister hired a personal trainer and tried body shaping, but we'd see each other and laugh at the fruitlessness of trying to escape.

Gradually, I began to take on her mannerisms, a standing slouch with knees turned in, hat pulled low over the brow. My clothes no longer matched and my hair was often ratty. Late at night, I sucked my back teeth. Increasingly, my blouses had spots where the breasts had stood like a ledge to catch any food that dripped. A napkin in my lap was useless. Food never made it that far.

"I used to think Mama was just sloppy with those stains all over her shirts. Now I see there's nothing you can do."

My baby sister was laughing as her breasts laid across the kitchen table. "I thought the personal trainer would help, but now look!" She stood up, looking just like my mother, with a muscular, masculine edge. "I bulked up even more."

We laughed at our flight from mother. I was trying to outrun her mind and my sister her body.

■ One day when I was fifteen, an old woman came to the front door. She stood there staring vacantly at me with a small suitcase in her hand. The blue car in the driveway pulled off, and a man ducked down over the steering wheel. The woman didn't speak, and we spent a few minutes staring at each other. I tried to speak, but opening my mouth created a vacuum and her face rushed into my chest. We continued to stare, and our faces kept spinning back and forth until the edges were blurred and our two faces became a single three-dimensional head. This was my dead grandmother, *my* mother's mother, who died when she was ten. I didn't need any introduction—my face was hers. It was like looking through a time tunnel with a mirror at the other end. I called to my mother in the kitchen and, when her face appeared, we became a three-dimensional hologram that floated with the same genetic imprint.

My mother opened the screen door and let her in. Without a word, she led us to the basement and closed the door. I still don't remember any words. We sat and looked and blinked and cocked our heads from side to side, as children do the first time that they look into a mirror and discover an image that moves with them. My grandmother reached into her suitcase and pulled out a book. The suitcase was small, like a weekend bag, of real leather, not leatherette, scratched and scuffed. The dust was wedged so deeply into the ripples that it had a gray mottled effect. The corners were badly beaten and in some spots the leather had completely worn off. The handle was shiny from use. She turned the book over on her lap and handed it to me. *Interior Decorating*. I didn't understand what she meant. Was she a decorator? Did she want me to learn decorating? But this was the only gift she had to give, coming so fresh from the asylum.

Eventually, my mother called for us to come upstairs. The man in the blue car had returned. I followed my mother back to the kitchen and studied her profile as she leaned over the stove, her face waxy from the heat and her lips stretched tightly over her teeth.

"I thought you said my grandmother was dead," I asked, narrowing my eyes.

She turned and looked at me full in the face, in a way to let me know the subject was closed. "Yes, that's what I said."

Biographical Notes

YOLANDA BARNES is a writer living in Los Angeles.

TAMMIE BOB's story "The Match (Blessed Is the Match)" won both an Illinois Arts Council Literary Award and the Daniel Curley Award. She is working on her first novel, *Playing by Ear,* from which both of the stories in this volume have been taken.

TERRI BROWN-DAVIDSON has a Ph.D. from the University of Nebraska, an M.F.A. from Vermont College, and has published widely. She has received Yaddo and Millay Colony fellowships, an AWP Intro Award, and additional honors.

EILEEN CHERRY, a Ph.D. candidate in the department of performance studies at Northwestern University, has published short fiction in anthologies and literary magazines.

LORETTA COLLINS received an M.F.A. in poetry from the Writer's Workshop at the University of Iowa, where she is currently a Ph.D. candidate in twentieth-century American and Caribbean literature. Her dissertation is titled "Trouble It: Rebel Soundscapes in the Caribbean Diaspora." Her poems have appeared in *TriQuarterly, The Missouri Review, Black Warrior Review, Quarterly West, The Antioch Review,* and other journals. Her poetry manuscript is titled "Fetish."

PAGE DOUGHERTY DELANO has published poems in many literary journals, including *Kenyon Review, Prairie Schooner,* and *Western Humanities Review.* She has been awarded fellowships to the Virginia Center for the Creative Arts and the Blue Mountain Center.

Having been an activist among coal miners in the 1970s, she now lives in New York City. She is currently teaching at Montclair State University and completing a Ph.D. in English.

STEVE FAY works as a naturalist at Forest Park Nature Center in Peoria Heights, Illinois. His work has appeared in several journals over the years, and he holds degrees from Monmouth College, Western Illinois University, and Warren Wilson College.

WILLIAM LOIZEAUX's nonfiction book *Anna: A Daughter's Life* was published in 1993. He has also published stories in *Carolina Quarterly, Massachusets Review,* and *TriQuarterly.*

DEAN SHAVIT is completing a Ph.D. in writing at the University of Illinois at Chicago. He has published poems in a number of literary journals, including *Another Chicago Magazine, Chicago Review, Poet Lore, Poetry East, Private Arts,* and *TriQuarterly.* The poems in this volume come from his manuscript "Dressing the Dead."

CASSANDRA SMITH has a B.A. from the University of Michigan, an M.A. from Howard University, and an M.B.A. from the University of Southern California. She has been a museum curator, university professor, director of marketing, and security guard. She works odd jobs to support her writing habit.